A Surprisingly Fluffy Bird

To Janice
Good Luck with
your adventures

Jenny Chapman

This book is dedicated especially to
Algy's oldest and dearest friends
Val and Michael

And to all the other kind friends
who have supported Algy's adventures

Algy sends you all
A Surprisingly Fluffy Hug

With extra special thanks to Mali

Jenny Chapman

A Surprisingly Fluffy Bird

AN SITHEAN PRESS

The Tales from the Adventures of Algy series is supported by Algy's web site for children, where young readers can learn about Algy's world, add their own pictures and poetry, ask questions, download colouring sheets, look up words in Algy's online dictionary, and discover many other fluffy surprises.

www.adventuresofalgy.com

Published by An Sithean Press, an imprint of MacAvon Media
Achnaha House, Kilchoan, Acharacle PH36 4LW Scotland (UK)

ISBN: 978-1-910637-01-2

Contents

～◎ Chapter 1 ◎～
Voices in the Mist

"Land Ahoy!" cried Algy, as loudly as he could, but the lonely sound of his voice just drifted away on the wind, until it was lost in the dense, swirling mist.

Algy knew that it was still very early in the morning, but instead of getting lighter, the day seemed to be growing darker and darker as the mist got thicker and thicker. He could barely see the water beyond the edge of his little raft, and the sky had vanished entirely.

Algy took a big, deep breath and tried again, for the one thousand and thirteenth time.

"Land Ahoy! Oh, please land, please be Ahoy!"

And for the one thousand and thirteenth time, there was not a single reply.

Algy listened very carefully. He could hear the wind whispering and sighing as it swept through his feathers, and the waves splish-sploshing as they washed up against the battered old crate that was his raft, but like so many times before, that was all. Or was it?

He leaned out into the wind, and listened again, even more attentively. Was that a sort of rhythmic rumbling roar in the distance? Algy concentrated…

There definitely was a new sound: a new and insistent sound. It had a pounding, crashing kind of rhythm to it, and it kept repeating, over and over and over again

Kerrrrrrrr-BOOM ker-swish-Swosh
CRASSSHHHHH kerrrrr-BOOMMMM
Ker-swishhh-swoshh Swozzle-wash
swizzle-wash swizzle-wizzle

Kerrrrrrrr-BOOM ker-swish-Swosh
CRASSSHHHHH kerrrrr-BOOMMMM
Ker-swishhh-swoshh Swozzle-wash
swizzle-wash swizzle-wizzle

Algy was both excited and alarmed. A new sound must mean that there was something different out there at last, but was it something good? He was not at all sure. He tried to peer through the grey mist in the direction of the noise, but all he could see was more mist.

Algy called out again, more hopefully this time.

"Land Ahoy! Hello! Hello Land! Are you Ahoy? Hello!"

"What's this? What's this? What's this?" quacked a harsh voice, which seemed to come from somewhere close to Algy's foot, beyond the front of the raft. "What's all this noise and fuss about? What's going on here?"

Algy almost jumped out of his feathers in amazement. He had not heard any voice except his own for longer than he cared to remember.

"Hello! Hello! Hello!" Algy shouted eagerly, waving his wings at the swirling mist. "Are you there? I mean, where are you? Are you really there? I can't see you."

"Of course I'm here," snapped the voice crossly. "What an idiotic question. What you mean is, are you there? And if you are there, why are you there and what are you doing? What do you mean by making all this noise and disturbing my sleep?"

"Oh, I'm sorry," said Algy, "I didn't realise. You see, I'm lost. Completely and utterly lost… at sea!"

"Well of course you're at sea," snapped the voice, and it sounded even more annoyed than before. "We're all at sea here. Where did you suppose you were?"

"But you don't understand," said Algy miserably, "I'm not supposed to be at sea. I don't belong at sea. I'm a fluffy bird, not a seabird. I live on the land – the lovely, warm, dry land, where the sun shines and the other birds sing in the trees. And I'm lost and cold and tired and wet and thirsty and hungry, and an awfully long way from home. At least, I think I am. I'm totally lost."

"Lost?" quacked the voice. "What's lost?"

"I am lost," wailed Algy, "and I'm also very cold, and horribly wet."

"I said 'What's lost?' not 'Who's lost?'" quacked the voice. "What do you mean by lost?"

"I don't know where I am," said Algy. "I don't know how I got here and I don't know where my home is and I don't know where this is, or anything."

"Sounds like utter nonsense to me," snapped the voice. "Far too much fuss and commotion. Go on about your business and leave me in peace. Good day!"

"But I need help," cried Algy. "Won't you help me? Please!"

This time there was no answer.

"Hello," called Algy, leaning out into the mist. "Are you still there? Hello? Hello?"

4

Algy craned his neck towards the place where the voice had come from, but he could hear nothing except that repetitive distant roar. Still it kept on pounding

Kerrrrrrrr-BOOM ker-swish-Swosh CRASSSHHHHH kerrrrr-BOOMMMM Ker-swishhh-swoshh Swozzle-wash swizzle-wash swizzle-wizzle

but now it seemed to be slightly louder than before. Either Algy was getting nearer to the sound, or the sound was getting nearer to Algy, and he didn't like the thought of either very much.

"Yoooooooou follow meeeeeeeeeeeeeee," crooned a new voice softly behind him.

Algy tumbled over backwards in surprise, and then very cautiously pulled himself around. A beautiful silky head was bobbing up and down in the water by the edge of his raft, gazing at him gently with large brown eyes.

"Yoooooooou follow meeeeeeeeeeeeeee," it sang.

"Gracious!" gasped Algy. "I mean, hello! Ummm… How do you do?" Algy was startled and confused, and not at all sure what to say. The creature's head was as large as Algy's body, if you didn't include his legs and his wings, but it had a kind, friendly-looking face, with pretty whiskers on each side of its mouth.

"I beg your pardon," said Algy, "but could you help me please? I'm so lost and tired, and I'm cold and wet and hungry. I don't know where I am or where to go or how to get there, and there's that pounding noise in the distance that keeps going

Kerrrr rrrr-BOOM ker-swish-Swosh CRASS SHHHHH kerrrrr-BOOMMMM Ker-swishhh-swoshh swozzle-wash swizzle-wash swizzle-wizzle

Kerrrr rrrr-BOOM ker-swish-Swosh CRASS SHHHHH kerrrrr-BOOMMMM Ker-swishhh-swoshh swozzle-wash swizzle-wash swizzle-wizzle

and I think it may be dangerous. Could you please assist me?"

"Follow meeeeeeeeeeeeeeeeeee," sang the kind face. "Follow meeeeeeeeee. Can you swimmmmm?"

"Oh… no," said Algy sadly. "No, I can't swim. I'm not a water bird, I'm just a fluffy bird." He was afraid that the creature would vanish again when it realised that he couldn't follow it through the water, but there was no point in telling a lie.

Algy thought for a moment. "But I can probably paddle the crate with my wings. I'll try."

"Follow meeeeeeeeeeeeeeeeee," crooned the kind face, and it suddenly disappeared.

"Oh, please wait!" cried Algy in alarm, "I can't see you!"

The smooth, glistening head popped back out of the water and looked at him again.

"I swimmmmmm underneeeeeeeeeeeath," it crooned softly, "but I will sing to yoooooou. Follow meeeeeeeeee. Follow meeeeeeeeeeeeeeeeeeeee."

≈≈ Chapter 2 ≈≈
Beware the Black Rocks!

Algy started to paddle his old wooden crate, trying to guess which direction the friendly creature was taking beneath the waves. He swayed from side to side, paddling first on the right and then on the left, hoping that this would keep him on course. It was horribly hard work, and in no time at all his wing feathers were drenched, and felt heavy and sticky with sea salt.

The mist was still as thick as porridge, and Algy could not see where he was going. There was nothing out there but mist: mist ahead of him, mist behind him, mist swirling wetly all around him. Algy wondered whether he was making any progress at all. He tried to listen for his guide's soft voice, but all he could hear was that worrying sound again

Kerrrrrrrr-BOOM ker-swish-Swosh CRASS SHHHHH kerrrrr-BOOMMM Ker-swishhh-swoshh swozzle-wash swizzle-wash swizzle-wizzle

and it was definitely much louder than before.

Algy stopped for a minute, to rest his aching wings and to listen for the singing voice without the distraction of his splashy paddling. Suddenly, he heard a new and very different kind of voice: a raucous sort of screaming, shrieking screech.

"Beware! Beware! Beware!" it shrieked. *"Black Rocks! Black Rocks! Beware the Black Rocks!"*

"What black rocks?" shouted Algy in alarm. "What's out there? What's happening? What should I do?"

"Follow meeeeeeeeeeee," sang the voice of the friendly creature, from somewhere in the mist on his left. "Follow meeeeeeeeeeeeeeeeeee."

"Black Rocks! Black Rocks! Beware! Beware! Beware!" screamed the other voice, and the piercing

shriek seemed to come from Algy's right-hand side, in the same direction as the

Kerrrrrrrr-BOOM ker-swish-Swosh
CRASSSHHHHH kerrrrr-BOOMMMM
Ker-swishhh-swoshh Swozzle-wash
swizzle-wash swizzle-wizzle

Algy leaned as far over to his right as he dared, trying not to upset the raft. Thrusting both his wings into the water, he started to paddle as fast and as hard as he could, desperately trying to steer himself away from the frightening sounds.

His guide was singing again, a little fainter and further away this time, but still crooning the same soft song. "Follow meeeeeee. Follow meeeeeeeeeeeeeeee."

Algy paddled and paddled and paddled. He paddled till his back ached and his head ached and even his beak ached, but the more he paddled, the harder it was to keep going. His wings grew heavier and heavier as they became more thoroughly soaked in sea water, and before very long he could not manage to lift them at all. He still wasn't sure whether he was making any progress, but he just had to rest.

Letting his sodden wings droop limply down onto the raft, Algy slowly looked around. He had been so absorbed in his paddling that he had failed to notice the mist lifting as the sun rose higher in the sky. The air was still damp and hazy, but the view was clearer now. On three sides, Algy could still see nothing but ocean; the water stretched out and across and away, until it faded into the distance. But on his right-hand side, he could see something horribly different: a huge, spiky, black mass rising straight up out of the sea.

The Black Rocks! Algy stared at their jagged edges in horror. Massive waves were thumping and pounding against the rocks with terrific force, throwing water and foam high into the air before it came crashing back down. And there, on the top of the highest crag, surrounded by white sea spray, stood a tall black bird, scrawny and thin, with enormous outstretched wings. As he strained his eyes to see more clearly, the bird tipped its head back and Algy heard that shrieking call again:

"Beware! Beware! Beware! Black Rocks! Beware! Black Rocks! Beware!"

At the same time, he heard a thundering

Kerrrrrrrr-BOOM ker-swish-Swosh
CRASSSHHHHH kerrrrr-BOOMMMM
Ker-swishhh-Swoshh Swozzle-wash
swizzle-wash swizzle-wizzle

The two sounds mixed up together made a ghastly din of alarm.

Kerrrr**rrrr**-**BOOM** *Beware!* ker-
swish-Swosh *Beware! Black Roc…*

CRASSSH *Beware!* **HHHH** kerrrrr-
BOOMMMM *Black Rocks!* Ker-swishhh-
Swo… *Beware! Beware!* shh Swozzle-wash
swi*Black…*zzle-wash swizzle *Rocks*-wizzle
Beware!

The gaunt black bird kept on screaming and shrieking;
the sea kept on hammering and battering the rocks.
Neither the sea nor the bird rested for a moment, and it
looked as though they would never stop.

There was no doubt now where the danger lay, and
Algy knew that he must not wait a split second longer.
Unless he paddled very fast indeed, he would be caught
up in the sea's powerful tow and hurled up into the air
until he came crashing back down, smashing into a
million smithereens on the terrible Black Rocks.

He plunged his aching wings back into the water,
but at that very moment his raft lurched and twisted
suddenly sideways. Algy keeled over and started to slide
into the sea.

"Help!" he cried hysterically, as the crate lurched
again. "Help! Help! Help! Help!" But no help came.

Algy grabbed hold of the rough wooden edges of the old crate, and clung on perilously while it rocked and tossed. The current had caught hold of it and was starting to pull him towards the deadly rocks. Algy was terrified, but he knew that if he wanted to stay alive he would need to keep absolutely calm and do exactly the right thing. Even though he could now see land, he could barely lift his wings and they were far too wet for him to attempt to fly in such a dangerous situation. He didn't stand a chance of escaping that way. His only hope was to paddle for his life. Otherwise… smithereens!

Quickly but carefully, Algy eased over onto his front and stretched himself out flat across the floundering crate, to avoid being toppled into the water. Then, with his toes tucked behind one edge, he extended both his sodden wings as far as he could, across the raft and into the water on either side. It was even harder to paddle in this position, but it was his only chance. If he sat up again he would be thrown into the sea, and if he failed to steer clear of the rocks he would certainly be smashed into thousands of tiny pieces.

So Algy lay on his front and paddled. He paddled as fast as he possibly could: faster and faster, harder and harder, feverishly trying to drive his raft away from the terrifying Black Rocks. He puffed and panted and gasped with the effort; every part of his body started to ache.

Even breathing was painful, but he kept on going and didn't pause for an instant.

From time to time as he frantically paddled, Algy thought that he could hear the faint sound of his guide's voice, singing somewhere in the water ahead of him: "Follow meeeeeeeeeee. Follow meeeeeeeeeeeeeeeeeee." Or was he just imagining it?

Algy clenched his beak tightly, and kept on going... until, after what seemed like a horrible eternity of painful paddling, he realised that the world had grown much quieter. The awful sounds of the Black Rocks were gradually fading away.

When he felt reasonably sure that the rocks were some distance behind him, Algy stopped paddling and slowly manoeuvred himself up into a sitting position. His body was so stiff and exhausted that he barely had the strength to remain upright, and every single feather ached. He tried to focus his attention on the movement of the raft, but his mind kept wandering. All he wanted to do was go to sleep… if only he could just curl up and sleep for a week or two… "No!" he told himself. "Don't be stupid! That's dangerous. Stay awake! Stay awake!"

Although his brain was foggy, Algy knew he must make sure that he had escaped from the deadly pull of the currents around the Black Rocks. With a huge effort, he concentrated on the movement of the raft again. The old crate was rocking and swaying gently with the motion of the sea, but that was all. There was no more lurching and tugging. He was safe – at least, he was safe from the perils of the Black Rocks. But where was he now? Algy looked around.

He was a little further out from the coast than before, and on his right he could now see a series of rocky bays and inlets, with rugged hills rising up behind them. But in front of him – right there in front of him – lay something he had been hoping to see for such a long, long time; something he had feared he might never see again. There was a wide band of glistening, silvery sand, stretching out along the edge of the land like a pale fringe between the hills and the sea. Algy could hardly believe his eyes: it looked exactly like a beach.

And just there in the water ahead of his raft, Algy could see the sleek head of his guide looking back at him. "Follow meeeeeeeeeee. Follow meeeeeeeeeeeeeeee," the soft voice sang. "Not farrrrrrrrrrr. Not farrrrrrrrrrr."

"I'm coming," Algy called, but he noticed that his voice seemed strangely feeble and weak.

Algy kept his eyes fixed on his friend until the silky head vanished beneath the water again, and then he looked beyond, at the beautiful, sandy beach. Maybe it was some kind of sea-mirage, or perhaps he was simply dreaming. He looked again; it was still there.

After such a long time at sea, the sight of land and a welcoming beach was almost too much for Algy. He felt faint and peculiar, and wondered whether the horror of the Black Rocks and the desperate effort of paddling had affected his mind. He had heard of castaways going crazy at sea; perhaps it had happened to him! But it really didn't seem to matter now… All he had to do was paddle a tiny bit further, and then he would be safe. Then he could go to sleep…

So, with the shimmering beach in view, Algy began to paddle once more, but much, much more slowly than before. He was no longer sure of what he was doing, and his wings were so painful that he could only move them stiffly and hesitantly, one at a time. But slowly his raft glided forward, and very soon he could hear a new sea-sound, much more friendly than the terrible pounding and crashing of the Black Rocks. As he began to crumple forward, Algy thought that he felt his little raft lurch again, and a sudden sensation of cold, drenching wetness, but he was far too tired to care. It didn't matter now; there was a beautiful, sandy beach ahead, and a soothing lullaby of breakers rolling gently up onto the safety of the shore. It sounded so reassuring and restful… Go to sleep… go to sleep… go to sleep…

⇜⇜ Chapter 3 ⇝⇝
Flotsam or Jetsam?

Little by little, and exceedingly slowly, Algy began to return to consciousness.

It had been so quiet and peaceful in his deep, dreamless sleep that he really didn't want to wake up. But what was all that noise? It was anything but quiet now! There was some sort of cacophony going on. Algy couldn't see what was happening, but he could hear voices – several different voices, all talking with a strange accent – and it sounded as though they were very close by.

Where was he? Everything seemed to be wrong. His eyes were stuck half closed with some sort of gloop, but so far as he could tell by peeking through his sticky eyelids, there was nothing out there but a greyish-white sky. And he felt wet – horribly, soakingly wet.

As he gradually became a little more alert, Algy realised that he must be lying flat on his back. He could breathe all right, but even his head seemed to be utterly drenched, and it felt as though his face feathers were glued to his beak. Algy tried to move his wings, but they were so dreadfully heavy and stiff that he couldn't lift them at all. He tried again, but it was no good. He just didn't have the strength to move.

The voices that had woken him were still jabbering loudly, somewhere not far from his head, and they were arguing with each other. It sounded as though they might not be friendly, so it would be wise not to draw attention to himself. As he wasn't able to move, and could certainly not escape in a hurry, Algy decided to lie absolutely still and listen to what the voices were saying. Perhaps their conversation would give him a clue about what had happened. Algy concentrated on listening:

"Flotsam!" shouted one unpleasantly raucous voice.

"Jetsam! Jetsam!" yelled another, that sounded almost the same.

"Flotsam! Flotsam! Flotsam!" shouted the first voice.

"Jetsam! Jetsam! Jetsam! Jetsam!" yelled the second.

"Absolute nonsense," crackled a third voice, with a deep, sharp sound. "Nothing of the sort. It's a bird. Just a soggy dead bird."

"Flotsam! Flotsam!" shouted the first voice again.

"Old Eachann is right," rasped a fourth voice, which despite its harsh tone sounded kinder than the others. "It's a poor drowned bird. Are you sure that it's dead?"

"In that state?" crackled the third voice.

"It's maybe nothing but a wee bundle of old rags," squeaked a tiny little giggling voice from somewhere near Algy's feet.

"Poke it and see," crackled the third voice, sharply.

Algy felt a sudden prodding in his middle, and realised with horror that the voices must be talking about him. He tried to open his beak to call out to them but, like his eyes, his beak seemed to be stuck half-closed.

"I'm afraid it really is dead," rasped the kinder voice. "We must leave it to the sea."

"Flotsam! Flotsam! Flotsam!" shouted the raucous voice that Algy had heard first. "Flotsam! Flotsam! Flotsam! Flotsam!"

"Jetsam! Jetsam! Jetsam!" yelled the second one.

"Away with you," rasped the kinder voice, with a tone of authority. "Away back to your fishing and leave us in peace."

Algy could hear the flapping of wings around him, and then a more distant yell of "Flotsam! Flotsam! Flotsam!" He continued to listen, but the voices had stopped.

Algy wondered whether he was alone. He was feeling dazed and confused, and only half awake. Flotsam, jetsam, drowned, bundle of rags… for a while he could make no sense of what he had heard. He was so terribly tired; all he wanted to do was sleep.

He was just about to drift off into unconsciousness again when he felt a strange sensation – a weird, wet, tickling sensation, as though something very squishy was squelching against the feathers on his head.

Algy tried to pull himself together. He really mustn't go back to sleep; he must force himself to wake up. Something was definitely wrong here.

He listened again, and realised that all the time that the voices had been jabbering there had also been another noise – a continuous, persistent noise in the background. It seemed to be getting slightly louder:

It faded away. Then again:

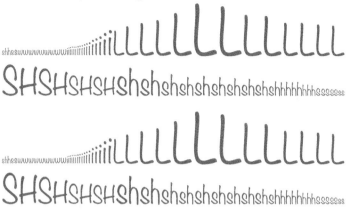

And the squelchy thing that was tickling his head was rubbing against him in rhythm with the last part of the noise, and then moving away again as the noise faded: around him and away, around him and away…

Flotsam, jetsam, drowned… All at once, the words began to make sense.

Drowned, flotsam… the sea! Now he remembered. The raft… the awful, frantic, painful paddling… the Black Rocks, the shrieking bird… the strange singing guide who kept disappearing… the terrible effort to reach the beautiful beach up ahead…

Algy didn't think that he was drowned yet; he was almost certain that he was still alive, although he couldn't be entirely sure. But if he was still alive, maybe he wasn't going to stay that way for very much longer!

"We must leave it to the sea," the kinder voice had said.

"Oh, no!" thought Algy. "The sea!"

In an instant Algy guessed what had happened. He must have been thrown off his raft by the turbulence of the breakers near the shore, and washed up onto the beach by the incoming tide. Perhaps he had hit his head when the raft overturned, or perhaps he had just collapsed from exhaustion. He had probably been lying there for hours, unconscious. And now… the tide was coming in again!

Algy concentrated on the sensations around his head. That was it! There was sea water washing around his head with the rhythm of the waves, and something else too – something swirling about in the water, tickling him.

"Leave it to the sea!" Definitely not! He was not going to be left to the sea if he could help it!

Making an enormous effort, Algy focussed all his willpower and energy on trying to sit up, and… Nothing! He was stuck. He tried again, and… still nothing.

Algy couldn't move. Suddenly, a wave of disgusting, salty water surged right over his head, and then drained slowly away. He choked and spluttered and choked and coughed and choked again… and sat bolt upright! The shock of being half drowned had achieved what he had failed to do before. And it had also washed his head, in a nasty, sticky, salty sort of way.

For the first time since he had regained consciousness, Algy found that he could open his eyes and his beak. Frantically, he looked all around. His vision was still blurry, but he could see as much as he needed to. He was sitting in shallow water, surrounded by masses of swirling seaweed. Behind him lay the ocean, in front he could see a wide expanse of sand, and behind that a series of large mounds that looked like sand dunes, stretching all the way across the back of the beach.

Algy looked down at himself. His wings were limp and utterly sodden, and his feathers were matted and stuck together with pieces of seaweed and salt. No matter how hard he tried, he could not shake them. One thing was certain: he would not be flying anywhere just now!

His body was a mass of aches from top to toe, and even the slightest movement was painful, but he couldn't see any injuries, and nothing seemed to be actually broken. He tried to wiggle his toes. It wasn't easy, but he could just about do it. His toes wiggled.

Algy gazed at the beach. It was mainly fine sand, with rocks jutting out of it here and there, but in the distance near the dunes there was a long, dark line of seaweed running all the way across from one side to the other. Algy guessed that it marked the place which the last high tide had reached. He knew that not every high tide would reach the same spot, but it was safest to assume the worst: after all, the next tide might be even higher!

shhssuuuuuuuuuuuuuiiiiiiiiiiiiiiiLLLLLLLLLLLLLL
SHSHSHSHShshshshshshshshshhhhhhhhsssssss

The water gushed in again, twisting more sticky seaweed around his legs. The tide was definitely coming in fast: he must move without delay, or he would be drowned after all.

He couldn't fly, but could he walk perhaps? That was the next thing to try, so, very gingerly, Algy attempted to stand. He bent his legs backwards, and slowly twisted himself up into an awkward kneeling position. Then, leaning forward onto the tips of his wings, he tried to push himself upright… but his feathers were so heavy with salt water and sand, and his muscles so weak from the strain of paddling, that as soon as he tried to stand up he toppled over, down into the seaweedy water again with a loud, squelchy splash. Hopeless!

sshhssuuuuuuuuuuuuuiiiiiiiiiiiiiiiLLLLLLLLLLLLLL
SHSHSHSHShshshshshshshshshhhhhhhhsssssss

There it was again, and each time he heard it, the water washing round him was a little deeper and the waves running up the beach advanced a little further. There was absolutely no time to lose, and he could think of only one way left to get away from the incoming tide. He would have to crawl.

Algy slowly pushed himself back up on to his knees and leaned forward into the water, supporting himself on his aching wings. The wet sand sank beneath his weight, sucking him down, and it was very difficult to pull himself free. But when it's a question of drowning or not drowning, a fluffy bird can do remarkable things. So, with a huge effort, Algy started to crawl through the swirling water on his wings and knees, dragging his feet clumsily behind him.

At first he made no progress at all. When each new wave washed in around him, it pulled him back as it returned to the ocean, dragging his knees deep down into the waterlogged sand. One crawl forward, one slurping, sucking tug back…

But Algy observed that not every wave reached as far up the beach as the last one. Although there wasn't a regular pattern, some waves seemed to be much stronger than others, and it was those strong ones which made progress impossible.

Algy decided that what he needed here was strategy, not just strength. Watching the sea very carefully out of the corner of his eye, he moved forwards only when the waves were gentle and weak, and stayed still when they were stronger. That was the way to do it: wait for the little waves and then ease his right knee forward, left knee forward; right knee forward, left knee forward; right knee forward, left knee forward…

This technique seemed to work quite well, and as Algy gradually crept through the shallow water he began to notice that some of the weaker waves were no longer managing to reach him. He was advancing up the beach!

As soon as he realised that he was gaining ground, Algy felt a great deal stronger and more confident. He lifted his head and gazed across the sand at the dunes. He told himself that if he just kept his eyes fixed firmly on those dunes, and carried on crawling when the waves were not too strong, everything would be all right.

And sure enough, before very long, Algy found that he was crawling across firm, damp sand: he had escaped from the water. Now the going was a little easier, because the waves could no longer slow him down and drag him back.

Algy stopped for a moment, and tried to brush the sticky sand off his feathers with his beak.

ShhsswwwwwwwwwwiiiiiiiiiiiiiiLLLLLLLLLLLLLLLL
SHSHSHSHShshshshshshshshshshhhhhhhhsssssss

He looked quickly over his shoulder, and there were the waves, close behind him again, chasing him up the beach, trying to catch him.

So on he went. It was a horribly slow and painful business, but he was sure now that he could make it, if he could just keep crawling: right knee forward, left knee forward; right knee forward, left knee forward; right knee forward, left knee forward; right knee forward, left knee forward…

～ Chapter 4 ～
The Great Wall of Seaweed

Algy had no idea how long it took him to crawl across the sand, but eventually he noticed that he had almost reached the long dark line of seaweed.

Now that he was closer he could see that it wasn't a line at all; it was an enormous bank of tangled kelp and other sea vegetables heaped up in a revolting, rotting mess. It ran all the way across the beach in front of him, for as far as he could see: a solid, slimy wall of seaweed. Algy had never seen anything like it before and, to make matters worse, the smell coming from it was disgusting.

Algy looked at it in dismay. The bank of seaweed was piled up much higher than his head, and it seemed to be very wide too. After his long struggle up the beach he could hardly face the thought of trying to cross that horrible stinking mess, but he had to get to the other side, because he would not be safe from the incoming tide until he did so. Algy peered along the seaweed wall in both directions, hoping to find some gap or break in the barrier, but he couldn't see any way through. He would just have to climb over it.

So Algy took a deep breath and crawled right up to the edge of the seaweed. Holding his breath for as long as he could, he tried to scramble up the steep side of the seaweed bank, but it was so amazingly slippery that he could get no grip on it anywhere. He quickly backed off again, to breath some fresher air and study the problem. He needed to get hold of something firm that he could use to pull himself up.

Spotting the end of a solid stem of kelp that was sticking out of the bank about half way up, Algy advanced again, and reached up with his beak to grasp the stem. Trying very hard not to breathe, he attempted to haul himself up the slithery pile, holding onto the stem with his beak while he climbed with his wings and feet. But the seaweed was far too slippery; he just skidded on the slimy surface, and slid about in every direction except up. Feeling sick from the stench, he accidentally let go of the kelp stem and dropped back down onto the sand with a painful bump.

"Ouch!" shrieked a very small voice from beneath him. "Get off, can't you? Why don't you mind where you're going?"

Algy jumped and rolled over several times, away from the stinking wall. He had not seen or heard any sign of another creature since the voices around him in the water had vanished, and he was exceedingly startled.

He stared at the spot where he had fallen, but at first he could see no one there. Then he noticed a tiny scuttling movement on the sand, right at the base of the seaweed bank. It was a little orange crab, and it was waving its claws at him angrily.

"I'm terribly sorry," said Algy. "I slipped. I didn't know you were there. Are you hurt?"

"Hurt?" snapped the crab, in its very small voice. "How could I be hurt by some great, hulking creature bouncing about on top of me? Hurt? Of course I'm hurt."

"I'm really very sorry," said Algy. "It was an accident. Is there anything I can do?"

"Go away," snapped the crab. "Just go away. And mind where you're going next time."

"Are you sure you're all right?" asked Algy. "I'm so sorry I hurt you."

"Stupid, clumsy creature," snapped the crab. "Of course I'm all right. I'm talking to you, aren't I? What do you mean by gallivanting about the place jumping on people?"

"I was trying to get across this huge wall of seaweed," said Algy. "I fell."

"Idiot," snapped the crab. "Stupid, clumsy idiot. Can't do it. Of course you fell. Can't be done."

"Oh," said Algy. "Ummm… well, is there any other way to get to the other side?" He thought it unlikely that an angry crab would be willing to help him, but it was worth a try.

"Stupid," snapped the crab. "Stupid straight-ahead creatures!" It snorted with a tiny little rasping sound. "Always going forwards instead of sideways. Stupid!" And it scuttled back into a small hole beneath the rotting bank of kelp.

"Sideways?" called Algy.

The crab stuck its head out again, and gestured with its claws. "Lateral thinking, lateral thinking," it snapped, waving its claws from side to side. "Think sideways, idiot. Stupid straight-ahead creature!"

The crab tapped one of its legs on the ground rapidly, with a tiny drumming sound.

"And mind where you're going!" it snapped, and vanished.

Sideways… Algy turned his head obediently from side to side and studied the enormous wall of seaweed stretching out along the beach. He could still see no break in the mass of kelp on either side. Was the crab just making fun of him?

Trying to see exactly what lay in each direction, Algy noticed that the light was growing very dim; it seemed to be almost twilight now. That was worrying. He was afraid to stay out overnight in this strange land: perhaps fierce, fluffy-bird-eating beasts might roam the beach in the night, or the next tide might be exceptionally high and he would be washed back into the sea. He had to cross the tideline and find a safe place to sleep before it was dark.

Algy looked sideways once again, first to the left, and then to the right. On his left, he could see all the way along the wall of seaweed, right up to the point where the beach ended in a massive pile of rocks. There was definitely no break in the seaweed in that direction, and the rocks looked awfully difficult to climb. In his weakened state he couldn't possibly manage such a climb before nightfall.

On his right, the beach extended too far for him to see all of it clearly, and so did the bank of seaweed. But, a little way along in that direction, there seemed to be a shining streak of wetness running down from the seaweed wall to the sea. It didn't look like a stream, just a broad band of very wet sand, shimmering in the last gleams of daylight. Algy couldn't see any gap in the seaweed at that point, but it was the only spot in either direction where something different was happening.

Algy leaned back wearily on the sand for a moment, wondering whether it was worth the effort of crawling along to inspect the wet sand.

The sound was surprisingly loud. Algy swung round, and there were the waves again. They had almost caught up with him!

That decided it. He would just have to hope that the crab had not simply been mocking him, and there really was some way through the seaweed wall.

So Algy turned and crawled sideways, following the bank of stinking seaweed to the right, but keeping a comfortable breathing distance away from the smell. All the time, he kept one eye on the waves running up the beach towards him. They were getting much too close.

He started to crawl faster, and soon reached the edge of the shimmering sand. His knees rapidly got wetter and wetter, and in a moment he was crawling through water again, but this time it wasn't sea water. It was a very shallow stream of fresh water, flowing out across the beach from the dunes to the sea. There was almost no depth to it at all, and where it crossed the sand it spread out to form the wide area of gleaming wetness that had caught his attention.

Pausing in the middle of the wet sand to study the seaweed wall, Algy gasped in surprise. Where the stream met the seaweed on the farther side, it had forced its way through the wall, towards the sea, creating a much deeper, narrower channel of water, with steep banks of seaweed hanging over it on both sides. A channel that he could crawl through!

Algy crawled forward quickly, into the running water, and started to push his way along the deep channel, through the massive wall of seaweed. The channel was only just wide enough for him, and he kept brushing against the slimy kelp on each side, but it was so firmly stuck together that it didn't budge or topple on him.

He reached the other side of the seaweed wall just as the waves were beginning to tickle its seaward edges. Not a moment too soon! Some of the more vigorous waves were already washing into the channel behind him, but luckily the gap was so narrow that very little water could get through.

On the far side of the seaweed, the stream had carved a wide course across the upper part of the beach, with miniature walls of sand at its edges that crumbled into the water with little sploshing sounds. It was quite shallow, except where it ran through the seaweed wall, so Algy had little difficulty in clambering out of the water and onto the dry sand at the side.

This sand was soft and warm and inviting, quite different from the hard, damp sand on the other side of the wall, but unfortunately the smell of rotting seaweed was too revolting to stay there, even for a moment. So Algy only paused long enough to catch his breath, and hastily crawled away as fast as he could.

As he moved towards the dunes, he gazed up at the great hillocks of sand that were towering over him now. They stretched all the way along the back of the beach, from side to side and beyond, further than he could see. The tops of the dunes were covered with tall, spiky grasses waving in the wind, but where the dunes met the beach it looked as though their edges had simply sheared away, leaving strange sand cliffs with long, dangling grasses and short twisted roots hanging out at all angles.

It was getting darker by the minute, and Algy urgently needed somewhere to sleep. The tops of the dunes looked a great deal safer than the beach, but he was too exhausted to try scrambling up those steep cliffs of sand. He looked around anxiously, worried that he would have to spend the night out in the open: there didn't seem to be any kind of shelter at all on the beach. Staring at the foot of the sand cliff immediately in front of him, he suddenly noticed what looked like a concealed opening, with many long grasses hanging down in front of it. It was difficult to see in the fading light, but there seemed to be a sort of dark hole there.

Making one final effort, Algy shook some more of the sticky wet sand from his feathers and started to crawl again. As he approached the cliff he could see that there really did seem to be a tiny cave in the sand, with a draping curtain of spiky grasses dangling across its entrance. It looked cosy and safe, but it was too dark to see inside it.

After his encounter with the crab, Algy was reluctant to enter the little cave unless he could be certain that it was empty. He couldn't see any scuff marks around the entrance, nor any other signs of occupation, but he wanted to make absolutely sure.

"Hello," he called softly into the mouth of the cave. "Is anybody there?"

There was no answer. He called again, "Hello in there. Is anyone at home? May I come in?" Still no answer.

Algy grabbed hold of a bunch of the strong grass stems and broken roots sticking out by the side of the entrance, and pulled himself through the grass curtain, into the mouth of the sand cave.

It was completely dark inside, but so far as he could tell, it was not very deep. He crawled a little further in, and felt around in the darkness with his wings. He could touch the walls on all sides, and the ceiling too, but it seemed to be big enough to accommodate him, and the sand felt stable and firm. It would do for one night.

So Algy patted some of the soft sand on the cave's floor roughly into the shape of a pillow, curled himself up on the ground, and with a huge sense of relief, almost immediately fell asleep. As he drifted off, he heard the muffled sound of the waves washing up against the far side of the seaweed wall at high tide. Now that he was safe, they sounded just like a soft, soothing lullaby again:

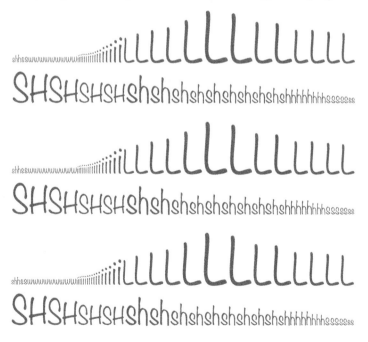

≫ Chapter 5 ≪
The Song of the Lark

"Good morning," piped a squeaky little voice. "And a braw, bright morning it is too."

Algy woke up with a start. Was that really a voice, or was he still dreaming? "Hello," he mumbled sleepily. "Is somebody there?"

"I canna tell," squeaked the little voice, giggling. "Will you come out and see?"

Algy slowly opened one eye, and then the other. Everything was dim and sort of orange-ish. His whole body was aching horribly from beak to toe, and he

38

seemed to be surrounded by sand. It made no sense to him. Where was he?

For a few minutes Algy just lay there on the soft bed of sand, wondering whether he was awake or asleep. Gradually he began to notice that there was light streaming in on him from one side, through a strange dangling curtain. It looked as though he was in some kind of tunnel or hole. Ah! Now it was coming back to him. The sand cave. He had crawled all the way up the beach and into a tiny sand cave at the foot of the dunes. He must have slept there all night – or perhaps even longer.

Flicking some of the sand out of his eyes, Algy turned towards the light, hoping to see who was outside, but compared with the dark interior of the cave the brightness out there was blinding. When he looked towards the light he couldn't see anything at all.

"Are you not coming out?" piped the little voice. "It's no' very safe in there."

"Just a moment," called Algy. "I'll be out in a minute." He sat up and started to rub himself all over, hoping to ease some of his many aches and pains, but there was almost no room to move. If he leaned his back against one sandy wall of the cave, his head touched the roof and his toes touched the wall on the other side. As he reached forward to rub his sore knees, his spiky hair brushed against the roof and a shower of sand tumbled down on his legs. Perhaps the squeaky voice was right, and the cave was not as safe as he had thought.

There was certainly not enough height to stand up in, so Algy rolled gently over onto his front, and carefully eased himself out through the grass curtain at the mouth of the cave, trying not to knock the walls as he went.

The light outside was dazzling. At first he could see nothing except whiteness, so he had to sit quite still, waiting for his eyes to adapt to the daylight. The sun felt pleasantly warm on his feathers, but there was a stiff breeze blowing and the air was cool and smelled of seaweed. As he couldn't see, Algy leaned back on the warm sand and listened to the sounds of the world around him. There was a repetitive swishling noise which sounded very familiar:

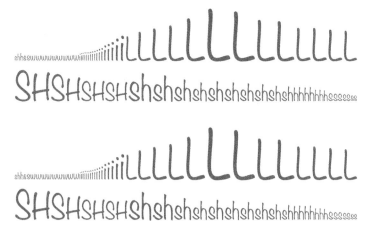

And way up above, somewhere high over his head, there was an entirely different kind of sound: a wonderful, glorious sound. It was a trilling song – a very long and elaborate song – and it was one of the loveliest sounds that Algy had ever heard.

Some bird up there was singing in a strange language – singing and singing and singing – with an unusually beautiful voice. Although he couldn't understand the words, the joyful melody made Algy feel suddenly happy and light-hearted. For a moment he completely forgot that his body was aching all over and he was lost in a foreign land, far away from home.

As Algy listened, the song started to change. The tune took a different, fluttering turn and slowly began to fade away until, all of a sudden, it stopped. Algy just sat there, entranced. He had never heard a song like that before. He waited eagerly, hoping that the singer would start again, but all he could hear was the constant, repetitive sound of the sea.

With his eyes still half closed, Algy peeped down at his body and wings. He was an incredible mess! There were hundreds of pieces of seaweed and clumps of sticky sand all over his body, and his feathers were filthy and matted. He tried to fluff himself up, but it was no good. Everything was stuck together. He attempted to preen and separate his sticky wing feathers, but they wouldn't budge, and they tasted very strongly of salt and other horrible things. He was obviously in urgent need of a long and extremely thorough bath!

"Good morning to you again," squeaked a shrill little voice, from among the roots of the dangling grasses beside Algy's head.

Startled, Algy swivelled round to see who was speaking, but there was no cause for alarm. It was a pretty little mouse, with unusually large ears and deep brown eyes. As it jumped down onto the sand and stretched itself upwards to look at him, Algy could see that its tummy was covered in beautiful, fine white fur. It was not quite like the mice he had known before, but it was undoubtedly a mouse.

"Good morning!" said Algy politely, smiling at the tiny creature.

"And how are you this morning?" squeaked the mouse, in a soft, slurred accent.

Algy knew that he ought to say "Very well, thank you," but it simply wasn't true. He was feeling terrible, so he decided to change the subject.

"I'm lost," he said. "I don't know where I am."

"You'll be a stranger here, then?" squeaked the mouse.

"Ummm, yes, I suppose so," said Algy. "I have certainly never been here before, and it does seem very strange. Can you tell me where I am?"

"You are in the Rustling Dunes," squeaked the mouse. "The Rustling Dunes by the Bay of the Sand Islands."

"Sand islands?" said Algy. "How can islands be made of sand?"

"It's no' the islands that are sand," squeaked the mouse. "It's the sand that the islands are lying in."

"Oh," said Algy, confused, and let the matter go for the moment. "What I really meant," he said, "is where are these rustling dunes? What land am I in?"

"Land?" squeaked the mouse, "This is the land of the Rustling Dunes by the Bay of the Sand Islands."

"Yes, I see," said Algy, "but what country is this? What country am I in?"

"I don't take your meaning," squeaked the mouse. "You should maybe ask someone else."

"Don't you know where you live?" asked Algy in surprise.

"Aye, to be sure," squeaked the mouse. "I live in the Rustling Dunes by the Bay of the Sand Islands."

Algy gave up. Rubbing his eyes once more, he looked around. His vision was clearing now, and he could see the beach and the sea without much difficulty. As he turned back towards the little mouse, he heard the beautiful voice of the trilling songbird again, coming from somewhere high above his head. Algy tilted his neck back and gazed upwards. The sky was a gorgeous colour, but he couldn't see anything in it. And then, way, way up in the blue, he spotted a dark, fluttering shape, almost too far away to see.

"Well, can you tell me who is singing that glorious song up there in the sky?" Algy asked the mouse. "I've never heard anything like that before."

"Aye, that would be Lark Lachlan," squeaked the mouse. "This is his favourite spot for ascending."

"Ascending?" said Algy. "What's ascending."

"Do you not know that a lark ascends?" squeaked the mouse in astonishment. "Surely everyone knows that."

"I'm not even sure what a lark is exactly," said Algy. "I have never heard the name before. But he certainly has a lovely voice."

"Aye, that he has," squeaked the mouse. "Well, a very good day to you, I hope you enjoy your stay." And it darted back into the cover of the dangling grasses.

"Oh, please wait a moment!" cried Algy.

The mouse's tiny head peeked out again, its large ears pricked up in Algy's direction.

"I'm sorry to trouble you," said Algy, "but I wanted to ask you something else. Could you tell me where I can get a good bath and find something to eat? I'm terribly hungry, and I really need a bath very badly."

"Aye, that you do," giggled the little mouse, covering its eyes with its hands. It peeked out at Algy through its tiny fingers, and giggled and giggled again.

"Where can I find some clean, fresh water that's deep enough to bathe in?" asked Algy. "I know there's water over there," he said, pointing to the shallow stream that had led him through the seaweed wall, "but it's very sandy and not really deep enough for a proper bath. Is there a deeper stream nearby?"

The mouse popped out from the grasses and looked up at Algy with its big brown eyes. It was doing its best to stop giggling, but Algy could see little tremors running up and down its furry body as it tried not to laugh.

"I bathe in the raindrops and the dew on the grass myself," it squeaked, "but the larger creatures use the Blue Burn."

"The blue burn?" said Algy, "That sounds more like a fire than a bath. What's the blue burn?"

"It's the Blue Burn that carries most of the water away from the hill, away down here to the sea," squeaked the mouse. "That there's just a wee silly burn," it added, nodding its head towards the stream through the seaweed wall. "You canna take a bath in that. But the Blue Burn is much grander. It has many fine places to bathe."

"Oh, you mean a river," said Algy. "That sounds fine. Where is it, please?"

"It's no' a river," squeaked the mouse, giggling again, "it's a burn. And it comes down away over there, by the end of the dunes." The mouse waved one tiny hand in the air, gesturing vaguely towards the far end of the beach behind Algy's back.

"Thank you!" said Algy. "I'll go and look for it."

"But will you no' have some seeds and nuts before you go?" squeaked the mouse. "I always keep a store."

"That's extremely kind of you," said Algy. "But I wouldn't want to deprive you."

"No bother," squeaked the mouse, and it shot off up the side of the sand cliff and vanished into the long grasses at the top. Suddenly, a round, brown nut came rolling down the cliff, and bounced near Algy's foot. Then another and another came tumbling down, and a shower of funny-looking seeds in different shapes and sizes. In no time at all there was a whole mound of nuts and seeds at Algy's feet.

The mouse's tiny head peered out of the grasses above. "Will you have any more?" it squeaked.

"Gracious, no!" gasped Algy. "Thank you ever so much, but that's plenty, really. Won't you come down and join me?"

"That I will," squeaked the mouse, and a moment later it popped out of a tiny hole at the base of the sand cliff, picked up a round nut with its tiny hands, and started to nibble it enthusiastically.

For quite a while there was no further conversation, just the sounds of nuts being cracked and seeds being happily munched, while Lark Lachlan continued to sing overhead.

Eventually, the mouse sat back on its long tail, and looked up at Algy again.

"I must be getting on," it squeaked, "I'll be seeing you…"

"Thank you ever so much," said Algy again. "I feel so much better now! But what's your name? You've been so kind, and I don't even know your name!"

"Catriona MacDougall," squeaked the mouse. "But they call me Wee Katie."

"Thank you, Katie," said Algy, "my name's Algy," but Wee Katie had already disappeared back into the dunes, and Algy was all alone on the beach once more.

∼⊚ Chapter 6 ⊚∼
A Dip and A Bob

The world looked entirely different after a good night's sleep and a hearty feast of seeds and nuts with a friendly mouse, and despite all his aches and pains, Algy felt positively cheerful. Lark Lachlan was trilling his joyful song again, in a sky of dazzling blue. All across the top of the dunes, the tall, spiky grasses were waving and rustling gently in the wind. And on the other side of the seaweed wall, the sea was twinkling and sparkling like a watery field of diamonds in the sunlight. It was a beautiful day.

Humming a little tune, Algy pushed himself up onto his feet and tried walking a few paces up and down on the sand. It had been a long, long time since he had last walked about on dry land, and it wasn't easy; he felt horribly shaky and unsteady. His legs were exceedingly stiff, and his knees were still very sore from crawling across the sand. But with a bit of practice he found that he could manage to walk a little, in a wobbly sort of way.

On such a lovely day, Algy felt even more ashamed of his disgustingly filthy state. He was very anxious to bathe himself as soon as he possibly could. Not only would he be unable to fly until he got clean, but he felt that a fluffy bird really ought to have bright, white, carefully preened and genuinely fluffy feathers on a beautiful day like this. Instead, he was a disgrace: a dirty, tangled mess!

Wee Katie had pointed to the end of the beach with the big rocks when she talked about the Blue Burn, but Algy could see no sign of any stream or river in that direction. It must be somewhere beyond the rocks. Brushing himself off a bit, Algy started to make his way very slowly along the top of the beach towards the rocks, singing quietly to himself as he went:

"Once, upon a stormy day,

  In a something land, so far away…"

"Something land, something land," he mumbled under his breath. "Lovely land, foreign land, shining land… Oh, bother… That's no good…"

"Are you talking to yourself maybe?" chirruped a voice in front of him.

Algy looked up. A small, slender, black-and-white bird was perching on the rocks ahead, its long tail bobbing up and down as it stared at him with a beady black eye.

"You'll be a stranger here?" it chirruped. "Do you always talk to yourself?"

"I was making up a song," said Algy. "I was trying to find the right word to fit."

"Is that so?" chirruped the bird, and it wagged its tail up and down many times.

"I'm looking for the Blue Burn," said Algy. "Can you tell me where it is?"

"Down that way," chirruped the black-and-white bird, wagging its tail vigorously towards the other side of the rocks. "Down that way."

"Is it far?" asked Algy.

"A dip and a bob," chirruped the bird. "Just a dip and a bob," and it flew up to the top of the highest rock and wagged its tail again.

"Thank you," said Algy politely, but the bird had flown away.

Algy gazed at the rocks, and he gazed at the sand cliffs. One way was hard and rough; the other was steep and slithery, in a sandy sort of way. Either way he might fall. He thought about it for a moment. If he fell down onto the soft sand at the base of the dunes he probably wouldn't hurt himself much, but if he slipped on the rocks he might sprain his ankle or bruise himself badly.

For a moment he wondered whether it wouldn't be simpler just to go back to the shallow stream and try to wash himself there. Perhaps he could bathe well enough to get his wings working again, and then fly over the top of the dunes to look for the Blue Burn later on. Now that he was close to the foot of the rocks, the distance back to the stream looked further than it had seemed while he was walking along singing to himself. He decided to try the sand cliffs.

Turning towards the dunes, Algy searched for a good spot to climb. It looked as though the edges of the dunes had collapsed onto the beach in stages – a bit here, then a bit there – creating all kinds of odd shapes. In some places the sand cliffs rose almost vertically from the beach to the top of the dunes, but in other places the cliffs rose up in sections, almost in large steps, with wide ledges and hollows of sand half way up, and lots of dangling grasses and bits of broken root sticking out at strange angles.

Choosing a convenient spot where the climb looked fairly straightforward, Algy started to scramble up the first part of a steep, sandy step. It was not as difficult as he had expected. His feet dug into the sand quite securely, and the long grasses were surprisingly strong – strong enough to take his weight when he tugged on them.

The sand felt warm in the sun, and although the climb was strenuous, it was not unpleasant. Algy started to hum again: he was almost enjoying himself!

He soon managed to clamber up to a point where the sand dipped down away from him into a large, scooped-out hollow, before rising up vertically again towards the top of the dunes. It felt lovely and warm in the sand hollow, sheltered from the cold wind that was blowing off the sea. Algy scrambled over to a soft-looking spot where he could lean back against the wall of sand, and rested there for a while in the sun, humming

"He fell into the water cold,

  He fell into the sea,

  He fell into the sea… fell into the sea…"

Sitting there in the warm sunshine, the thought of falling into the sea seemed like nothing more than a bad dream. Algy's eyes started to close, and he began to drift off to sleep; it was so comfortable on the soft sand, and he was so terribly tired from the efforts of the day before. His head started nodding gently as he murmured happily, "He fell into the sea… fell into the sea…".

"You'll not find the Blue Burn that way," chirruped a familiar voice.

Algy sat up with a start, wondering how long he had been dozing. The slender black-and-white bird swept past him through the air, with a strange, looping flight that dipped down and then up again. "A dip and a bob.

A dip and a bob," it chirruped, and swooped away out of sight again.

The sun did not seem to have moved very much, so Algy guessed that he had only had a short snooze, but the black-and-white bird was right: that was no way to find the Blue Burn! Rubbing his eyes sleepily, he got to his feet, gave himself a shake, and slowly started to scramble up the side of the dunes again.

The last stage of the climb was trickier, as there were fewer grasses to hold on to and the upper part of the sand cliff was steeper. He slipped a little, once or twice, but managed not to fall, and before too long he was pulling himself up onto a level patch of sand between two huge clumps of the long, spiky grasses that covered the tops of the dunes.

Somewhat out of breath, Algy rested there for a moment and looked back at the view. He could see now that the bay had not just one but several pale, sandy beaches, separated by rocky points that jutted out into the sea – including the one that he had decided not to climb. In the far distance, way out to sea on the left, he thought he could glimpse the terrible Black Rocks, although he couldn't be quite sure. And on the right there was a substantial headland close by, with some much higher areas of ground covered in rough, brown grass and bare rock, too tall to see beyond. Here and there, dotted about the bay, he could see many small, rocky islands – the Sand Islands, perhaps? But there was one thing he could not see: the Blue Burn!

Apart from the shallow stream that had led him through the seaweed wall, there was no sign of fresh water anywhere.

Suddenly, the black-and-white bird swept by again, turned, and landed on the sand close to Algy's foot.

"Still here?" it chirruped, wagging its tail.

It hardly seemed worth replying when the answer was obvious, so Algy just smiled.

"Not going to the burn after all?" it chirruped, cocking its head on one side.

"Yes, I am," said Algy, "but I still can't see any sign of it anywhere."

"Down there," chirruped the bird, wagging its tail towards the headland on the right. "Down there." And off it swooped again, dipping and bobbing as it flew back down towards the beach below.

Algy stood up. Except on the side where the sand cliffs descended to the beach, he was surrounded by the strange, tall, creamy-coloured grasses that covered the mounded tops of the dunes for as far as he could see. Determined to reach the Blue Burn, Algy started to weave his way through the huge grasses, which swayed to and fro, rustling almost constantly with a whispery sort of swishing sound as the stiff, spiky stems waved about in the wind. He was trying to aim for the headland, but the massive clumps of grass towered over him, and once he got right in among them he could no longer see where he was going. All he could see were more huge, spiky grasses on every side.

Turning this way and that, Algy stumbled around and about between the scratchy clumps, not getting anywhere very fast. But after blundering about for some time, he rounded what looked like just another clump, and stumbled out of the grasses onto a narrow, well-trodden, sandy path, heading in the right direction.

Algy paused, wondering what animal could have made such a path through the dunes in this strange land, and whether he would run into it. It was obviously much easier to walk on a clear, level path than to stumble about through the huge scratchy grasses, but he felt a little nervous. He resolved to keep a careful eye on what lay ahead – and behind!

So he started to walk along the path warily, looking forwards and backwards, backwards and forwards, concerned that some fierce fluffy-bird-eating creature might come sneaking around a corner at any moment. The path kept twisting and turning around the massive clumps of grasses, and Algy approached every bend very cautiously indeed. But, despite his fears, he met no one at all, and gradually the dunes began to level out until eventually they gave way to a large, flat area of short green grass – and there he saw the path-makers!

Algy laughed out loud; he had been worrying about a flock of silly sheep! "Hello sheep," he said happily.

"Baaaaaaa, baaaaaaa, baaaaaaa," answered the sheep in chorus, and nodded their black faces at him foolishly, munching all the time as they did so.

Algy had not met any black-faced sheep before, but they didn't seem to be very different from the other sheep he knew, except that they had fine curly horns.

"Do you know where the Blue Burn is?" he asked, just in case these sheep had more sense than their cousins overseas.

But the sheep just repeated themselves, "Baaaaaaa, baaaaaaa, baaaaaaa," and carried on with their grazing.

"No point talking to sheep," chirruped the voice of the slim little black-and-white bird, and there it was again, bobbing about on the grass in front of Algy, wagging its tail vigorously. "The burn's down there. Just a dip and a bob," and it wagged towards the headland.

Algy looked along the line of the wagging tail, and realised that where the green grass ended, only a short distance away, there was a gap before the ground rose up towards the higher areas of the headland. The Blue Burn must run through that gap.

"Thank you," said Algy. "Thank you very much."

"Just a dip and a bob," chirruped the bird, wagging merrily. "Enjoy your bath. I bathe there myself," and off it flew, dipping and looping back towards the dunes.

"Baaaaaaa, baaaaaaa, sheep," said Algy cheerily, waving at the sheep.

"Baaaaaaa, baaaaaaa, baaaaaaa," they replied in chorus, without looking up from their grazing.

Algy could hear Lark Lachlan singing up above, and pausing for a moment to look for him, he spotted the lark's small, dark shape fluttering high in the sky over the dunes. Algy smiled, and started to join in with his own song as he strode across the open grass:

"Twirling fast across the sky;
The bird on top
Was riding high, riding high, riding high…"

It was really no distance at all, and in just a few minutes more Algy was standing on top of the banks of the burn, which ran through a wide, deep, rocky channel it had carved out of the ground. On his left, the water looked bright and silvery as it danced and splashed its way through a rough course of tumbled rocks into the sea. But on his right, the burn looked bright blue.

∞ Chapter 7 ∞
The Blue Burn

Algy gazed down into the Blue Burn. The water was beautifully clear, and it looked fresh and inviting to a bird in need of a bath.

Although its rocky banks were steep in places, the burn itself was not very deep, and there were several flat, red rocks sticking out into the water on the far side; they would make ideal bathing platforms. There were also many large, rounded stones scattered about in the water, and a familiar black-and-white bird was wagging its tail on one of them, right in the middle of the stream.

"I found the Blue Burn," Algy called cheerily down to the bobbing bird.

The little bird cocked its head up at him. "Have we met?" it chirruped.

"Aren't you the bird who told me how to get here?" asked Algy, puzzled.

"That must have been one of my brothers," it chirruped. "We look alike." The bird wagged its tail briskly in amusement.

"Oh, I see," said Algy. "How do you do?"

"I do very nicely," chirruped the bird. "How about yourself?"

"I've come here to bathe," Algy explained, feeling uncomfortably aware of the filthy state of his feathers.

"Quite so," chirruped the bird. "Quite so, quite so," and it wagged its tail even harder. "A dip and a bob. And a good, long dip, I should say."

"Yes, I hope so," said Algy. "But how will I get down there? You see, I can't fly at the moment."

"Quite so," chirruped the bird again, looking Algy up and down and wagging vigorously. "Quite so. Can't fly. But there's a path. A sheep path. Up there," it chirruped, and pointed its wagging tail up the burn, away from the sea. "The sheep come down to drink."

"Oh, thank you!" said Algy. "That's just what I need."

"Quite so. A dip and a bob," chirruped the black-and-white bird. "A good, long dip and a bob," and it flew up into the air and away across the grass, with the same funny looping sort of flight as its brother.

Algy walked a little way along the banks of the burn, marvelling at how blue the water looked, and soon reached a place where the ground sloped down and a muddy little track led into the water, ending at a tiny beach churned up with the footprints of many sheep.

Tip-toeing through the mud, he waded carefully out into the stream. The burn was not flowing very fast and it was only as deep as his ankles, with a fine gravel bed for his toes to dig into. Algy found that he was able to make his way through the water without too much difficulty, holding on to the large stones one by one as he went.

He crossed to the other side, and waded along to one of the flat red rocks. The rock felt surprisingly warm: ideal for sunbathing after a bath. Holding onto the rock, first with one wing and then the other, Algy dipped his body down into the burn, over and over again, splashing the cold, fresh water all over himself as thoroughly as he could. From time to time he hauled himself out onto the rock to preen his feathers with his beak, and then got back into the water and started to wash again.

There are few things a fluffy bird enjoys more than bathing in fresh water on a beautiful, sunny day, so Algy soon started to sing again as he washed.

"A fluffy bird with hair of gold
    Perched on a branch,
    But lost his hold…"

he sang at the top of his voice, sending sprays of sparkling water cascading in every direction as he splashed enthusiastically.

"Ha-ha-ha-ha. Flotsam! Flotsam! Look at the flotsam!" a harsh voice suddenly yelled.

"Ha-ha-ha-ha. Jetsam! Jetsam! What a mess! Jetsam!" another voice answered.

"Ha-ha-ha-ha. Ha-ha-ha-ha," they yelled together.

"Flotsam! Flotsam!"

"Jetsam! Jetsam! Ha-ha-ha-ha. Ha-ha-ha-ha."

Algy had heard those raucous voices before. Pulling himself out onto the flat, red rock, he looked around. Two enormous seagulls with black backs were perching on another rock downstream, laughing at him with their mocking yellow beaks stuck high up into the air.

"Ha-ha-ha-ha. Look at the flotsam! It's alive!" shouted one gull.

"Ha-ha-ha-ha. That's a matter of opinion," yelled the other. "Filthy old jetsam! What a mess! "

"What kind of rubbish are you, flotsam?" shouted the first gull. "Never saw such a sight!"

"Ha-ha-ha-ha. Filthy old jetsam!" yelled the other.

"I'm a fluffy bird," Algy said quietly.

"A bird!" shrieked the first gull. "Ha-ha-ha-ha. Ha-ha-ha-ha. A bird! Don't make me laugh." It threw its head back and screamed with laughter. "Ha-ha-ha-ha. Ha-ha-ha-ha. Ha-ha-ha-ha."

"A bird!" taunted the second gull. "Ha-ha-ha-ha. Let's see you fly then, jetsam. Bet you can't fly."

"Well, no, I can't fly at the moment," said Algy. "But I'm still a fluffy bird."

"Ha-ha-ha-ha. I knew it," yelled the first gull. "Nothing but flotsam. Can't-fly flotsam!"

"Jetsam! Jetsam! Filthy-bird jetsam!" shouted the second, and they both started cackling again.

Algy was determined to enjoy his bath in peace. He turned his head away and gazed steadily at the bright blue water, humming quietly to himself while he pretended to ignore the gulls.

"Flotsam! Flotsam! Load-of-rubbish flotsam! Look out! It's trying to sing!" shouted the first gull, but Algy paid no attention.

"Jetsam! Jetsam! Ha-ha-ha-ha. Can't fly, can't sing," shrieked the second. But Algy looked the other way and took no notice.

"Flotsam! Ha-ha-ha-ha," yelled the first gull again, and jumped up into the air above Algy's head, cackling loudly at him, but Algy didn't look up.

"Oh, let's go and find some fun," shouted the second gull. "Nothing but rotten old jetsam here." And it too swept up into the air, and circled around Algy's head.

"Ha-ha-ha-ha. Ha-ha-ha-ha. Fluffy-bird flotsam! What a joke!" shouted the first gull, as it climbed up higher into the sky.

"Ha-ha-ha-ha. Filthy old jetsam! Can't fly, can't sing," yelled the other, as it joined the first gull.

"Ha-ha-ha-ha. Ha-ha-ha-ha. Ha-ha-ha-ha." The two huge birds circled slowly around together for a while, cackling as they flew, but Algy continued to ignore them, and before long their voices had grown much fainter.

Looking up to make sure that they were gone, Algy slipped quietly back into the water and continued his bath, splashing and preening until he had removed as much of the filth and seaweed from his feathers as he possibly could. Then he climbed out onto the warm, flat rock and stretched himself lazily across it to dry, shaking his feathers from time to time to get rid of the remaining water. Lying there contentedly in the warm sun, he started to sing again, in a sleepy kind of warm-afternoon sort of way:

"The wind began to roar and shout,
  The surf tossed foam and spray about,
  There wasn't any time to think,
  He tried to float,
  Began to sink…"

"Good afternoon!" snuffled a soft, lisping voice from somewhere above Algy's head. "It's a fine afternoon for a sunbathe, to be sure."

Algy looked up, and there on a peaty ledge near the top of the bank sat a large rabbit, twitching its nose.

"Hello!" said Algy. "Good afternoon to you."

"What's that you're singing?" sniffed the rabbit. "I don't think I've heard that song before."

"I'm composing a ballad," said Algy.

"A ballad!" sniffed the rabbit. "What's a ballad?"

"It's a very long song that tells a story," said Algy. "A song with lots and lots of verses. You know, in rhyme."

"You're making one up?" sniffed the rabbit. "Making up a new song? A new story?"

"I'm not making up the story," said Algy. "I'm just turning it into verses, and giving it a tune. It's the story of how I got here."

"How you got here?" snuffled the rabbit. "You don't belong here, do you? Oh," it sniffed, and rubbed its nose with a front paw, "I'm sorry. I didn't mean to be rude. But you're a stranger here, aren't you?"

"That's right," said Algy. "I arrived here yesterday. I wonder… Can you tell me where this is?"

"Where this is?" sniffed the rabbit.

"Yes," said Algy. "I've come a long, long way and I don't know where I am. Where is this?"

"This? This is the Bay of the Sand Islands," snuffled the rabbit.

"Ummm, yes," said Algy. "Actually, a little mouse did tell me that. But what I really mean is, what country am I in?"

"Country?" sniffed the rabbit. "What do you mean?" It wrinkled up its nose and twitched its whiskers.

64

"Doesn't anyone here understand me?" asked Algy, perplexed.

"I couldn't say," sniffed the rabbit.

Algy thought about this for a moment.

"Well, maybe you have a different word for it here," he said. "What I mean is, what is the name of the whole place here – all of the land, beyond the bay, beyond the sand dunes, even beyond those hills. What is the name of the whole place?"

"I don't know what you mean," sniffed the rabbit. "But I haven't travelled far myself. You should maybe ask a traveller."

Algy thought again. "Well, perhaps you know the name of the sea," he said. "Does the sea have a name?"

"Certainly," sniffed the rabbit. "This is the Sea of the Western Isles. You can see many of the islands from the Far View Rocks," and the rabbit waved his foot again, this time at the big mass of the headland beside them.

Algy began to despair of finding out where he was. Western Isles? West of what? "Are there Eastern Isles too?" he asked.

"I wouldn't know," snuffled the rabbit. "I've not travelled far myself."

Algy gave up. It was much too pleasant an afternoon to worry about a problem he obviously couldn't solve at the moment, so he leaned back on the warm rock and spread his wings out to continue drying.

"What's your name?" snuffled the rabbit.

"Algy," said Algy. "What's yours?"

"Ruaridh Gilleasbuig Alexander Fitzroy Hector Iain Cattanach MacLean," sniffed the rabbit, "but it's not my fault. You can call me Ruaridh."

"But that's a magnificent name!" exclaimed Algy. "I wish I had a wonderful name like that. Algy is such a silly, short, fluffy sort of name."

"Algy sounds fine to me," sniffed Ruaridh. "You're lucky. It doesn't take you all day to explain it to folk. Why don't you come up and join me?"

Algy didn't really want to leave the comfort of the warm rock, or get his feathers dirty again by perching on the peaty ground, but it seemed very rude to refuse. Reluctantly, he got to his feet, clambered up the steep bank, and sat down beside the rabbit.

"It's good to see someone new," Ruaridh snuffled. "Will you be staying long?"

"I don't know," said Algy. "I don't really know what to do. I'm lost, you see, and a very long way from home."

"Lost?" sniffed Ruaridh. "What's that?"

"I don't know where I am, or how to find my way back home," said Algy.

"That's a shame," snuffled Ruaridh. "You should maybe ask someone."

"Who could I ask?" said Algy.

"I wouldn't know," sniffed Ruaridh. "But you could maybe try the Singing Place. If you sang your song up there, they'd be sure to hear you. You should maybe ask someone up there."

"The Singing Place?" said Algy. "What's that?"

"It's a place for singing," snuffled Ruaridh. "It's away up there by the top of the Far View Rocks." The rabbit turned round and gestured towards the far end of the headland. "It's a fine place, to be sure. And they are always wanting new songs – new stories and new songs."

"That sounds interesting," said Algy. "Perhaps I'll try that."

"You'll need to finish your song first," sniffed Ruairidh. "And you'll need to talk to Roni."

"Who's Roni?" asked Algy.

"The Keeper of the Rocks," snuffled Ruaridh. "She minds the rocks up there. You'll need to talk to her first."

"All right," said Algy, "but how will I recognise her? Is she a rabbit too?"

Ruaridh snuffled and twitched with laughter. "A rabbit!" he chuckled. "No, she's not a rabbit! Roni is a raven. A huge black raven. If you go over to the Singing Place she'll be sure to find you. But it's too late for that today."

"Well, I haven't actually finished my song yet," said Algy, "so that's all right. But where can I stay tonight?

Is there somewhere safe nearby where I could sleep tonight?"

"I'd be glad to offer you a room," snuffled Ruaridh, pointing his nose at the round hole in the peaty bank behind them, "but that's maybe not very practical. Where do you usually sleep?"

"In a tree," said Algy.

"Oh," sniffed Ruaridh. "That's a wee problem, then. There are not many trees near here." He wrinkled his nose and twitched his whiskers up and down for a moment or two. "There's a battered old elder bush just up the way there," he sniffed, and gestured with one of his furry front feet towards the rough ground that rose up to the headland. "You could maybe try that. It's not very far."

"Thank you," said Algy, "I will."

"I'll be leaving you now," sniffed Ruaridh. "I have to be getting the tea."

"The tea?" said Algy.

"Mouths to feed, mouths to feed," snuffled Ruaridh, twitching his whiskers. "See you later." And he turned around and jumped up onto the level grass behind them.

"Oh, please wait a moment," called Algy. "I wanted to ask you…"

The rabbit paused and looked back.

"Are there any dangerous creatures here?" Algy asked. "Anything I need to know about?"

The rabbit shuddered. "Don't be asking that!" he snuffled. "Just be alert. Always alert! Keep an eye up above in the day, and down below in the night. Be sure to watch the ground in the night! Always alert!" And he lolloped away quickly, his tail bobbing up and down like a ball of white fluff bouncing across the rough grass.

"Thank you again," Algy called after him, and leaned back on the soft, warm, peaty bank beside the rabbit's home. He was feeling very sleepy and it was tempting just to stay there, but the sun was already sinking low in the sky. "Always alert! Be sure to watch the ground in the night!" Algy didn't like the sound of that at all.

Slowly he got to his feet, and shook himself vigorously. His feathers felt dry and fluffy at last, and he wondered whether he could fly. Hopping up onto the grass at the top of the bank, Algy tried flapping his wings a bit. They still ached terribly, and it was a huge and painful effort to lift himself off the ground. He fluttered a very short distance then fell back down, feeling like a foolish chick who was trying to fly for the first time. Perhaps it would be better to wait till tomorrow.

Looking around for the bush that the rabbit had mentioned, he spotted it almost immediately, just a short distance away. Its branches were bare, and it stood out starkly against the hillside like a twisted white skeleton.

Half fluttering, half walking, Algy made his way across the rough grass to the bush. There was a tumbled pile of large stones beside it, providing some protection from the wind but very little other shelter. Many of the branches were completely dead and stripped of their bark; they shone like ghostly limbs in the fading light. The whole bush had a strange and eerie appearance, and Algy did not care for it. It hardly looked like a safe perch for the night, but there was no other sleeping place to be seen.

He fluttered up onto one of the lower branches and inspected the bush more closely. Some parts of the bush did appear to be alive, but it was evidently too early in the year for leaves, as the living branches had only the tiniest of leaf buds on them. There was nothing to hide behind there. Then, right in the centre of the bush, Algy spotted a sort of scooped-out wooden hammock, formed where a massive, ancient branch had split right up the middle and spread apart. It was just about his size. It would have to do!

So Algy tucked himself tight into the heart of the old elder bush for the night, with his back and sides wedged firmly into his wooden hammock. Nervously, he tried to sleep, keeping one eye on the sky and one eye on the ground… Always alert!

～❧ Chapter 8 ❧～
Plog the Frog

Algy woke up with a start, his eyes snapping open. It wasn't exactly dark, but it wasn't exactly light; he guessed that it must be just around dawn. And there was a noise – the sort of noise that might be made by something creeping about very quietly on the ground nearby. He listened carefully. There was definitely a noise: the faintest sort of rustling sound, and maybe even the hint of a wheeze made by some creature breathing. Or was he imagining it?

Algy kept very, very still, and listened as attentively as he could. Yes, there it was again: a very soft rustling. He could hear the sound quite clearly, but it was impossible to tell what was causing it; perhaps it was only a sheep, or Ruaridh the rabbit out looking for breakfast.

Turning his head warily to one side and then to the other, Algy attempted to look at the ground, but the sides of his wooden hammock were too high. All he could see were the bare, ghostly branches of the old bush, and the pale dawn sky overhead. He tried to sit up very quietly, but he was wedged into his bed so tightly that it was impossible to move without attracting the attention of whoever was out there.

All of a sudden there was a bright leaping flash of a long white throat hurtling wildly towards him, and the longest, sharpest claws he had ever seen flying straight at his face with terrific speed. Algy shot straight up vertically into the air without a second's thought, banging his head and wings on several branches as he passed, and leaving a shower of fluffy white feathers drifting down gently behind him to the ground below.

He hovered in the air above the old elder bush, quivering, and peered down at his attacker. A dark, pointed face with perfectly round black eyes was staring up at him from the highest branch of the bush. The creature had a long bushy tail and looked rather like a small, dark-coloured fox, but no fox could climb with such agility or had such terrifying claws! From a safe distance the creature seemed quite beautiful, with its lush, dark fur, pretty face and ears, and its long, creamy throat, but for a fluffy bird the only safe distance was definitely a long way off the ground!

Algy was feeling far too shaken to remain hovering up there above the fearsome animal; he looked around desperately for somewhere to land where he might be reasonably safe. He could see that the headland was covered with many bare, rocky outcrops, which would at least make good lookout points. Without looking back, he flew as far as he could manage, and chose an exposed area of rock on higher ground, in a spot which seemed to have a clear, unobstructed view to every side.

Dropping down onto the highest point on the rock, he perched there, shaking all over. As he watched nervously for any sign of the animal approaching, he realised that he must have been flying again – for the first time since he had left home! If he hadn't been feeling so shaken he would have been delighted, but under the circumstances it was all he could do to stop trembling like a dried-out leaf in the autumn wind.

"What's the matter?" chirped a little voice behind him. "Are you all right?"

Algy leaped straight back into the air. He was in such a jittery state that the tiniest sound was enough to frighten him out of his wits. But this time it seemed that he was safe. Looking down at the rock where he had been resting, it was obvious that the voice belonged to a delicate little brown bird, so Algy fluttered back down again, feeling rather foolish.

"I'm sorry" said Algy. "I've just had a terrible scare. A horrible dark animal with a long white throat and terrifying claws leaped at me when I was half asleep. I only just got away, and I don't seem to be able to stop shaking."

The little bird shuddered. "Oh," it whispered, "you must have met one of the Dark Ones."

"It was the narrowest escape I have ever had," said Algy. "Do you think it will come after me?"

"Probably not just now," chirped the bird. "Not now that the sun is rising."

"What was it?" asked Algy. "It didn't look quite like a fox."

"They're not foxes," whispered the bird, "though they're just as cunning." The little bird shuddered again.

"Do they only hunt at night?" Algy asked fearfully.

"No," whispered the bird. "Mainly at night, but sometimes in the daytime too. They can run like a fox, climb trees like a squirrel, and swim – although they don't care much for the sea. And they'll eat anything… everything… fur… and feathers…" The little bird shuddered again. "I think I'll be going," it chirped nervously. "I really can't stop here," and it flitted off to another rock not far away and perched there, anxiously looking this way and that.

Algy also looked this way and that, and every other way that he could see, but there was no further sign of danger. The sun had just risen up from behind the ridge in the distance, and as the first rays fell on his face he started to feel a little safer. Slowly relaxing, he shook out his feathers, and rested there in the morning sunshine, keeping a sharp lookout all around.

After staring at the landscape for some time, Algy began to remember what he was really there for. The fright of his encounter with the dark animal had completely driven it from his mind, but slowly he started to think about finding the Singing Place, and wondered which direction he should take. From his perch he could see nothing but more rocky outcrops, with rough, boggy land lying low in the gaps between them. There was a particularly wet area close by, where pools of blue water were shimmering among pale tussocks of reeds and grasses. Looking at the water made him feel thirsty, so checking very carefully that there was no dark, furry creature with frightful claws to be seen, he flew down to the pools for a drink.

As he cautiously approached the water, hopping from tussock to tussock to avoid getting wet and dirty again, Algy heard a strange sort of croaking voice, apparently reciting a poem:

"The fish lay on the seaweed wall,
Whence all but he had fled;
While far away the tiddlers small
Had safely gone to bed.

So scaly and sublime he stood,
As he surveyed the storm;
A creature of piscean blood,
A shining silver form.

The waves rolled on – he would not go
Without a lobster's word;
But lobsters, who lived down below,
Were very rarely heard.

The fish called out 'Oh lobster, say,
If I may leave my post.'
He knew not that the lobsters lay
Far off along the coast.

'Speak, lobster!' once again he cried,
'I want to have my tea.'
But only rolling waves replied
From far across the sea."

"Hello," Algy called out. "Good morning!"

"What? What? Who's there?
Are you aware
You must declare
Your presence here?"

Algy peered down into the tangle of leaves and old grasses that lay across the boggy edge of the water. The voice seemed to be coming out of the bog, but he couldn't see anyone there.

"Who are you?
I think you're new," croaked the voice.

"I'm Algy," said Algy, "and I'm new here, yes. Who are you? And where are you? I can't see you."

"That's Plog," chirped the little brown bird, who was now perching on one of the grassy tussocks.

"Plog the frog,
  The Bard of the bog,
  Sits all agog,
  His mind in a fog;
  Croaks his old rhymes
  With a voice like a hog."

Algy tried not to laugh, but he couldn't prevent himself.

"There's nothing amusing about the name Plog,
  And every good frog must live in a bog."
croaked the invisible voice.

"I'm sure you're right," said Algy towards the bog. "Well, I'm pleased to meet you, Mr Plog."

"Not mister, just Plog.
  Not a man! I'm a frog!" croaked Plog indignantly.

"I beg your pardon," said Algy politely.

"Those cheeky birds don't know it,
But I really am a poet.
They all try to make fun of me,
But that's just their own idiocy."

"Oh," said Algy, "I'm sorry to hear that," and he stared again at the place where the voice seemed to be coming from, trying to spot the frog.

"I ask you, is it reasonable?
It isn't even seasonable,"

croaked Plog, and very slowly, two bulgy eyes and a wide mouth emerged from the bog with a sort of gurgling, bubbling sound.

"My name is Fergus Ferguson,
The son of Og the frog;
His name was Fergus Ferguson,
But always known as Og.

A frog must have a rhyming name,
And so they called me Plog,
Upon the day that I became
The poet of the bog."

"I like to make up rhymes and verses myself," said Algy, reassuringly. "I think it's a fine thing to do."

The frog hopped out onto a dense patch of soggy, tangled grass at the edge of the bog, and stared at Algy.

"But you're not an amphibian,
  You're not even a reptilian."

"Well, no," said Algy. "But fluffy birds can make up rhymes too, you know."

"Know? No! You're much too slow,
  You must keep time,
  To make a rhyme," croaked Plog.

"And there's no time to lose,
  There are rhythms to choose;
  It's a question of metre,
  And nothing is neater."

"I see," said Algy politely. "I'll do my best."

"You may do your best,
  But I'll do the rest," croaked Plog.

"Now, what is the matter?
  I've no time to chatter."

"I'm trying to find the Singing Place ," said Algy, "but I don't know where it is. I've lost my way."

"Lose your way
  And you're bound to stray."

"That's right," said Algy. "So can you please tell me which direction to take from here?"

"The proper direction,
  Is my suggestion," croaked Plog.

"There's no point asking Plog," chirped the little brown bird on the rock. "He doesn't know. He never leaves the bog, except when Old Eachann carries him, and then he keeps his eyes shut."

Algy turned towards the little bird. "Carries him? Why does he do that? And who's Old Eachann?"

"Creatures who are curious
  Will come to no good end,
  Other folk won't trust 'em
  So they will not find a friend."

"Don't mind him," chirped the little bird, "he just can't stop making rhymes. Old Eachann is an old grey heron. Plog can't hop far, so if he needs to travel – to sing one of his poems, maybe – Old Eachann carries him. But Plog hates it. He usually refuses to go."

"I should think he does!" exclaimed Algy. "A heron carrying a frog..."

"The heron is a hunting bird
  The frog should treat with caution,
  Or else he's liable to be
  The heron's dinner portion."

Plog croaked with some feeling.

"Yes indeed!" Algy agreed. "I think you're very brave to let him carry you."

"Old Eachann would never hurt him," chirped the little brown bird. "He knows better than that."

"It isn't what he knows that counts,
'Cause if he needs a snack,
He may provide a ride from which
I never will come back!"

"Poppycock!" chirped the bird. "You know Old Eachann won't hurt you. You just like to make a fuss."

After his recent encounter with a hunting creature, Algy felt a considerable amount of sympathy for Plog, but as he didn't know Old Eachann he thought it might be wise to change the subject. "Perhaps you know the way to the Singing Place," he said to the little bird.

"Of course I do," chirped the bird. "I sometimes sing there myself."

"Why didn't you say so before?" said Algy.

"You didn't ask me," chirped the bird.

"Well, could you please direct me?" asked Algy.

"If you like," chirped the bird. "Follow me." And it flitted over to the top of the next rocky outcrop and looked back at Algy. "Are you coming?"

"Yes, yes," called Algy. "Please wait."

He looked down at the frog, who was goggling at him.

"Goodbye," said Algy, "I hope we will meet again soon. We can have a nice conversation about poetry."

"Poetry is quite an art,
Reciting it is tricky,
You have to learn the words by heart
And some of them are sticky."

Algy was somewhat puzzled by this, but he couldn't spare the time to discuss the matter. "Well, I really must be going," he said. "Goodbye again," and he flew up into the air, towards the rock where the little brown bird had been perching a few moments earlier. "Where have you gone?" he called to the bird.

"Over here," chirped the bird, and Algy saw that he was now on top of another rock, some distance away.

"Hurry up," chirped the bird. "I can't stop here."

"I'm coming," called Algy, and flew on towards the bird, who immediately flitted away to a different rock.

And so they proceeded in short flights from rock to rock, apparently heading for one of the highest points on the headland. Each time that Algy flew towards the little brown bird it moved on again, always managing to stay one rock ahead.

Algy tried to make sense of where he was going, but the landscape seemed very confusing. There were many rocky mounds, covered in patches of rough grass and dry heather, with exposed rock on top, and a lot of marshy bogland lying low in between them. Whichever way he turned it all looked much the same, except for a few points which were significantly higher than the others. He could not see what lay beyond in any direction.

"Come along, come along," chirped the bird, from yet another rock. "I can't stop here."

So Algy flew on again, following the little bird, until

eventually it stopped on the top of the highest point of all, and waited for Algy to catch up.

Algy flew up to join the little bird and gazed around in astonishment. Suddenly he could see the sea, spread out in almost every direction. Far down below them the water was swirling and gurgling around dark rocks and massive rock pools, and in front of them the grassy headland gradually sloped down towards a rocky point which jutted out into the ocean. But what surprised him most of all were the islands.

Ruaridh the rabbit had said that you could see many islands from the Far View Rocks, but he hadn't dreamed there would be quite this many. There were islands everywhere: small, black, rocky islands close by, and large, mountainous, purple islands across the sea. There were even several pale blue misty islands, floating far away out on the horizon. The only spot without islands was behind him, where the rugged land stretched away until it met some very steep rocky ridges.

"There you are," chirped the little brown bird. "The Singing Place," and it nodded its head towards a large, flat rock, with edges like wide steps that led down into the rough grass. The rock lay on the opposite side of a narrow chasm, which plunged down steep black cliffs just in front of them to the pounding sea below.

Algy looked over towards the Singing Place, and saw that a large raven was perching there, watching them.

"You'll be Algy," rasped the raven in a loud, hoarse voice, which carried clearly across to them and probably far beyond. "I've heard about you. I am Roni, the Keeper of the Rocks."

Algy felt a little nervous. The raven did not look unkind, but she didn't exactly look friendly either.

"Off you go," chirped the little brown bird. "I can't stop here," and it flitted away again, back down to one of the lower rocky outcrops.

"Thank you!" called Algy, as the little bird left. "Thank you very much."

"Hop over here," rasped Roni the raven. "I've been waiting for you."

So Algy hopped. He hopped down from the rock at the highest point, and across the gaping chasm, trying not to look down as he did so. Then he fluttered over to the flat rock where the raven was waiting.

"This is the Singing Place by the Far View Rocks," rasped Roni. "I understand that you wish to sing. Is it a good song? Did you compose it yourself?"

"I don't know if it's a good song," said Algy, "but I did make it up myself. It's a ballad. A ballad about how I got here."

"I see," rasped Roni. "That might be interesting. You may proceed."

"You mean now?" asked Algy, surprised. "I wasn't expecting to sing quite so soon."

"Why not?" asked the raven. "Aren't you ready?"

"Ummm… I suppose so," said Algy hesitantly. "I wasn't quite prepared, actually, but if you really want me to sing now, of course I will."

He looked around. So far as he could see, there was not another creature within earshot, just himself and the raven, and a few seabirds attending to their business out on the nearest rocky islands. "Ummm, there doesn't seem to be anyone here to listen, though," he said, "except yourself, of course."

"They will come," rasped Roni. "They will come. Please sing," and she hopped over to a small rock some distance away and looked back at him expectantly.

"Please sing," echoed a small, fuzzy voice from somewhere near Algy's foot.

Algy looked down at the ground. A round, furry face was staring up at him, beaming. "Hello!" said Algy. "Who are you?"

"I'm Mr Voles," murmured the funny little animal, which looked something like a cross between a fat brown rat and a very large mouse, but without a pointy nose or a long tail. "Mr Voles."

"Delighted, I'm sure," said Algy kindly, as the droll little creature seemed to be so friendly. "I'm pleased to meet you."

"Pleased to meet you, pleased to meet you," echoed Mr Voles.

"Would you like to hear my song?" asked Algy. "I would be glad to sing for you."

"Sing it for me," agreed Mr Voles happily, and his smile got even bigger.

"All right," said Algy, "I will." He settled himself down on the flat rock at the top of the Singing Place and prepared to sing, taking a deep breath and throwing his head right back, with his beak pointing up towards the sky. But as he began to open his mouth, he heard the sudden shriek of familiar voices, calling from the rocks beside the pools down below.

"Flotsam! Flotsam! Look out! Flotsam at the Singing Place! Ha-ha-ha-ha. Ha-ha-ha-ha. What a joke!" yelled the first voice.

"Jetsam! Jetsam! Rotten old jetsam wants to sing! Got to hear that! Ha-ha-ha-ha. Ha-ha-ha-ha. Can't-sing jetsam! Ha-ha-ha-ha," shouted the second.

"Pay no attention," rasped Roni from her rock. "Please start your song."

"Please start your song, please start your song," murmured Mr Voles, creeping closer to Algy and climbing up onto his foot. Algy couldn't help smiling. He looked down at the grinning Mr Voles, then tipped his head back again, gazed up at the bright blue sky, and started to sing…

✺ Chapter 9 ✺
The Ballad of a Fluffy Bird Lost at Sea

Once, upon a stormy day,
Not long ago, but far away,
A fluffy bird with hair of gold
Perched on a branch,
But lost his hold.
And sad to say
(Truth must be told)
He fell into the water cold,
He fell into the sea.
He tumbled down into the sea;
That clumsy fluffy bird was me.

The wind began to roar and shout,
The surf tossed foam and spray about,
There wasn't any time to think,
He tried to float,
Began to sink.
Then suddenly a waterspout
Swept by and saved him from the brink
Of drowning in the briny drink:
It sucked him from the sea.
It snatched him boldly from the sea;
That drowning fluffy bird was me.

The day was dark, the clouds were black,
The spout spun on a frantic track,
Twirling fast across the sky,
The bird on top
Was riding high.
The thunderclouds began to crack,
And lightning bolts went flashing by:
The poor bird thought that he would die
And perish in the sea.
He thought he'd perish in the sea;
That wretched fluffy bird was me.

The waterspout rushed straight ahead,
The bird was shuddering with dread:
His future seemed so very short,
The fluffy bird
Was quite distraught.
As madly over sea he fled,
The waves were in his every thought;
The bird's predicament was fraught
With danger from the sea.
His life was threatened by the sea;
That frightened fluffy bird was me.

Then, all at once, the lightning flashed,
The sky burst open, thunder crashed;
The waterspout released its grip,
And soon the bird
Began to slip.
Back down into the sea he splashed;
Beneath the waves he took a dip
As frantically he tried to flip
Back up out of the sea.
He tried to jump out from the sea;
That frantic fluffy bird was me.

His leaping was to no avail,
The ocean had him by the tail;
Foul salty water filled his throat
When suddenly
He saw a boat
With battered mast, and tattered sail
Made out of some poor sailor's coat.
And there was something else afloat –
A bobbing raft upon the sea.
He saw a raft upon the sea;
That startled fluffy bird was me.

The boat was nothing but a wreck,
No soul was left upon its deck:
There was no sign of the crew's fate,
A story
Sorry to relate.
The bird struck out; he had to reach
The raft: it seemed to be a crate.
He wondered: would it take his weight
Upon the tossing sea?
A crate was rocking on the sea;
That struggling fluffy bird was me.

A lucky change in the sea's swell
Conveyed the drowning bird so well
That he was thrown against the raft
With so much force
He almost laughed,
And uttered an exultant yell
Of joy, to find himself so close abaft
A seaworthy and comfy craft:
A nest upon the sea.
He found a nest upon the sea;
That happy fluffy bird was me.

The floating crate was strong and sound,
Secured with tacks and wire around.
He grabbed hold of the rocking side
And quickly
Hauled himself inside.
Overjoyed that he had found
A raft upon the ocean wide,
He curled up happily and sighed,
Then rested on the sea.
The bird was safe upon the sea;
That rescued fluffy bird was me.

And thus, inside this floating nest,
The bird set forth upon the crest
Of waves, across the briny deep;
At times awake,
At times asleep.
Northwards, southwards, east or west?
He had no compass that would keep
Direction, so he had to sweep
With currents through the sea.
The currents swept him 'cross the sea;
That drifting fluffy bird was me.

At first the bird was full of hope;
He did not grumble, moan or mope,
But sailed along in jaunty style,
With happy heart
And cheery smile.
To pass the time, and help him cope,
He sang sea songs and shanties, while
He kept an eye out for an isle
Upon the deep blue sea.
He sought an island in the sea;
That hopeful fluffy bird was me.

But the ocean, cruel indeed,
Does not provide for birds in need.
He sailed for many a day and night,
And still no land
Came into sight.
Without supplies, he could not feed,
And could not get a drink despite
The water all around; a plight
Too common on the salty sea.
He could not find a drink at sea;
That thirsty fluffy bird was me.

Then, after many a tedious day,
The raft began to rock and sway;
The wind began to roar again,
The air was thick
With mist and rain.
The waves whipped up with frothy spray,
The raft was creaking with the strain;
The bird could only just maintain
His balance on the sea.
The raft tossed on the stormy sea;
That rocking fluffy bird was me.

The raft was pitching to and fro,
The bird hung tightly on, although
The crate was leaking water fast:
Could it withstand
The tempest's blast?
Hurtling with the mighty flow
Of waves across the ocean vast,
The fluffy bird held on, aghast,
In dread upon the sea.
He clutched his life-raft on the sea;
That frightened fluffy bird was me.

The wind with awful violence blew,
Across the sea the old crate flew,
Until at last the storm subsided,
But the raft
Had been divided
Into pieces, all askew,
When, by chance, it had collided
With a floating tree trunk, guided
By the currents of the sea.
The raft broke up upon the sea;
That shipwrecked fluffy bird was me.

The bird clung on to what was left,
And with manoeuvre swift and deft
He climbed onto the top of it,
To perch upon
A broken bit.
The bottom of the crate was cleft
In pieces; it was split
In two, but he could sit
On part of it, and float upon the sea.
The bird could still float on the sea;
That agile fluffy bird was me.

And so, across the briny foam,
The battered raft began to roam,
Carried by the wind and tide
Until it reached
The other side.
The bird was very far from home
When finally he met a guide,
And to that creature he applied
For help upon the sea.
He asked for help upon the sea;
That lonesome fluffy bird was me.

The kindly creature sang a song,
Which guided that poor bird along,
By huge black rocks, where every wave
Could smash a bird
Into his grave.
The undertow was very strong,
And though the bird tried to be brave
He feared his guide would fail to save
Him from the thrashing sea.
He thought his life would end at sea;
That fearful fluffy bird was me.

The waves crashed on the jagged rocks
With frightful noise and booming knocks
That threw the spray high in the air
Around a gaunt bird
Standing there:
A guard, whose awful shrieking shocks
Poor mariners, in grim despair,
Who offer up a final prayer
For rescue from the sea.
They ask for rescue from the sea;
That praying fluffy bird was me.

Then suddenly the old crate lurched:
The part where the poor bird had perched
Tipped up; the bird was sprawled
Across the rocking raft,
He bawled
"Oh help me, please," and madly searched
For sign of help, but was appalled
When no kind creature answering called ·
To guide him through the sea.
No help came to him on the sea;
That frantic fluffy bird was me.

And then, some way off to one side,
He saw his friendly singing guide:
That gentle creature who had led
With song, to show
The way ahead.
And so he paddled on, and tried
To follow where the creature sped
Beneath the waves, its silky head
Emerging singing from the sea.
Its head popped up out of the sea;
That paddling fluffy bird was me.

As vigorously as he could
He paddled that old raft of wood;
He paddled till his wings were sore,
Until he could not
Paddle more.
The singing creature, kind and good,
Led him to a sandy shore
That he had never seen before:
A gleaming beach beside the sea.
He saw a beach beside the sea;
That joyful fluffy bird was me.

But as the beach got ever nearer,
And his view of it grew clearer,
Faintness overcame that bird,
And though his spirits
Had been stirred,
And no sight could have been much dearer,
With a sigh, just barely heard,
The bird collapsed, without a word,
And tumbled down into the sea.
He fell again into the sea;
That senseless fluffy bird was me.

Some time then passed, or so he guessed,
And really you all know the rest.
The bird washed up upon the beach,
Unconscious, and then heard
A screech,
And felt a prodding in his chest;
A crowd had gathered round, their speech
Was argumentative, but each
Agreed to leave him to the sea.
They left him to the heartless sea;
That half-drowned fluffy bird was me.

And so I reached this foreign shore.
There is no point in telling more,
Because you know what happened then:
I crawled across the sand,
And when
I found a cave with grassy door,
I crept inside that sandy den,
And as I slept on land again,
The lullaby of swishing sea
Sang "You are rescued from the sea."
That lucky fluffy bird was me.

I hope that you've enjoyed this song,
And maybe learn to sing along.
This ballad was composed for you,
And every bit of it
Is true.
I wish that I could now belong
To this cold land, so strange and new,
To which, by some odd chance, I blew,
From far away, across the sea.
I can't go back across the sea;
A homeless fluffy bird you see…
Could this new place be home to me?

⚮ Chapter 10 ⚯
The Singing Place

The last notes of Algy's song drifted softly away on the wind, and for a moment or two there was no sound at the Singing Place except for the constant muffled roar of the sea around the rock pools far below.

A small crowd had gathered while Algy was singing, just as Roni had predicted, but they were all quite still. Not a creature spoke.

Suddenly, Ruaridh the rabbit bounced his way through the crowd and started thumping the ground vigorously with one of his back feet.

"Bravo!" he cried enthusiastically. "Bravo Algy! A fine song! Bravo!"

"Bravo! Bravo! Bravo!" squeaked a chorus of mice at the front, jumping up and down in excitement.

All at once, shouts of "Bravo! Bravo!" started to come from every side. Many creatures began to applaud: the birds flapped their wings together, the animals clapped with their paws or thumped their feet on the ground, and a pair of snakes hissed rhythmically as they swayed from side to side. The noise was almost deafening.

But the great black-backed gulls, who had flown up from the rocks to perch sulkily on the dry grass to one side, just continued to yell "Flotsam! Rubbish! Flotsam!" and "Jetsam! Can't-sing jetsam!" with their mocking yellow beaks stuck high up in the air.

"Don't mind them," sniffed Ruaridh, nodding towards the gulls. "Nothing pleases them."

"Nothing pleases them," agreed Mr Voles.

Algy stared at the applauding crowd, unsure of what he was supposed to do next.

"Listen!" rasped Roni. "Listen to Silvie," and she waved a jet black wing in the direction of the rock pools. "Silvie is singing to you."

Algy gazed down towards the rocks, where the sea was swirling in and out of the pools, and there, hauled out on a flat, black rock, was a long, gleaming blob of a creature, who seemed to be looking up towards them.

He could barely hear her song over the sounds of the sea, but he recognised her voice. It was the voice of the creature who had guided him to shore.

"Silvie wants to sing your ballad," rasped Roni.

"She led me to the beach," said Algy quietly.

"That's right," rasped Roni. "She's our coast-guide here. Every bay has its own seal guide."

"Really?" asked Algy. "Do they all sing?"

"Certainly," rasped Roni. "And when they aren't working, the seals gather together on the rocks and sing the stories of the folk they have rescued. Yours will make a fine story for a summer's night."

"A fine story," murmured Mr Voles, as he rubbed himself against Algy's leg.

"Thank you, Silvie," Algy shouted, as loudly as he could, flapping his wings vigorously at the seal. "Thank you very, very much! I wouldn't be here without you. Of course you can sing my song."

The seal waved a friendly flipper in the air, and turned away. With a strange undulating motion, she slowly wiggled and wobbled her awkward body across the rocks until she reached the edge of the sea, then slipped gracefully into the water and vanished.

"She has gone back to work," rasped Roni. "The guides can't rest for long."

As the seal slid into the ocean, Lark Lachlan flew up into the air from a patch of heather a little further down the hillside, and fluttered over to join them, warbling quietly as he flew. Perching on the rock seat beside Algy, he trilled a short song in that strange, soft language that Algy didn't understand.

Roni nodded her head, and looked at Algy. "Lark Lachlan wants to sing your song too," she rasped. "That's quite an honour. The Lark is most particular about his repertoire."

"But how did he understand it?" asked Algy. "I thought he spoke a different language."

"The Lark is a canny one," squeaked a little mouse at the front of the crowd. "He understands us fine, but he only sings in Gaelic."

"Only sings in Gaelic," echoed Mr Voles.

"With your permission, Lark Lachlan will translate your ballad into Gaelic," said Roni. "Then the whole world will hear your story each spring, when the Lark sings above the Rustling Dunes."

"That's wonderful," said Algy, with a big smile on his face. "Lark Lachlan has one of the most beautiful voices I've ever heard. I'd be thrilled to hear it."

"Thrilled to hear it," agreed Mr Voles.

Ruaridh nudged Algy with his nose. "You ought to say something," he sniffed. "They're waiting."

Algy glanced up at the crowd, and then looked down at his feet, where Mr Voles was washing his furry face. "Ummm..." he began, and paused.

Ruaridh nudged him again. "Go on," he snuffled.

Algy coughed. "Ummm… well, the first thing I'd like to say is that I'm very happy that you enjoyed my song. And that anyone can sing it if they'd like to. I'd be delighted, really I would."

"Bravo!" squeaked a young mouse.

"Bravo!" echoed Mr Voles, and his funny round face looked up at Algy with a reassuring smile.

"I'm so grateful for all your kindness," Algy continued, "and I'm also very glad and relieved to be here. It's wonderful to have been saved from the sea at last, and to have landed in such a beautiful place… even though it's awfully cold." Algy shivered as the sharp wind whistled through his feathers, and several of the mice giggled.

"I don't know where my home is, exactly," he went on, "but I think that it's far away from here."

"Bravo!" squeaked the little mouse again.

"Shhhhhh," rasped Roni sternly. "Be quiet."

"It's quite all right," Algy said kindly to the young mouse. He looked around at the crowd of faces watching him. "But to be honest," he said, "I don't really know where 'here' is, and I'm not sure what to do now. I don't see how I can go back home. I'm sure it's an impossibly long way, and I don't even know which way to go."

"Bravo!" squeaked the young mouse.

"Shhhhhh," rasped Roni again, in a hoarse whisper. "Don't be stupid. Be quiet."

"So I'd like to ask your advice," Algy continued, looking at the crowd, "and I'd also like to know exactly where I am."

"You are at the Singing Place by the Far View Rocks, overlooking the Bay of the Sand Islands," rasped Roni.

Algy turned towards the raven. "But doesn't this whole land have a name?" he asked. "I've asked several times, but no one seemed to know. Surely you know?"

"Know what?" asked Roni.

"The name of this land," said Algy. "What is the name of this land – the whole country, including the sea and the bay and the islands and whatever lies on the other side of those hills, and beyond? And whereabouts in the world is it? I completely lost my sense of direction when I was drifting on the sea."

"That would be a question for Old Eachann," rasped Roni, and she nodded at a stately grey heron who was standing at the back of the crowd.

"Old Eachann," she rasped, "may I present Algy? He is lost and has some important questions for you."

The tall heron stalked slowly to the front of the crowd, and all the other creatures fell back to let him pass. Pausing in front of Algy, he peered down from the top of his long, thin neck, and spoke in a strange, deep, crackling voice. "You are welcome, Algy. But I think you are asking the wrong question. However, as you are lost and looking for help, I will try to explain. We have

106

no name of the kind that you mean. We have only the names of the rocks and the bays, the mountains and the sea, the islands and the bogs, the burns and the lochans, the trees and the forests and the plants. Every thing has its own name, but we have no name for everything."

"Oh, I see," said Algy, who didn't see at all, really.

Old Eachann continued. "I'm not sure what you mean by whereabouts in the world, but I understand that you have travelled a long way, across the sea, and that you have not been here before. Perhaps things seemed different in the place that you came from. So I can tell you that here the days are very short and dark in winter, when the sun only brushes lightly across the top of the ridge before it goes back to sleep, and the nights are very short and light in summer, when the sun barely slumbers, but hovers out there in the distance, glowing red beyond the edge of the sea. Here it is never hot, but it is rarely very cold. The rain falls often, and the snow falls occasionally, but the wind blows most of the time. This is a land of sea water and fresh water, of silver light and salty air, of bright rainbows and dark clouds."

"Ummm… thank you very much," said Algy, who was feeling thoroughly bewildered, but couldn't think what else to say.

Old Eachann bent his long neck graciously in acknowledgement, and slowly stalked away again, back to his place behind the rest of the crowd.

"Why don't you just stay here with us, Algy?" snuffled Ruaridh, twitching his whiskers. "It may not be like the place that you came from, but it's a fine place."

"Of course!" rasped Roni. "Stay here with us! You can compose new songs for us."

"New songs for us," echoed Mr Voles.

"Rubbish! Flotsam! Rubbish! Go home!" yelled one of the black-backed gulls.

"Fly away!" snapped Roni sharply towards the gulls. "Away back to your fishing and leave us in peace. You have no business here." She turned back to Algy, and spoke more kindly. "We need new songs," she rasped.

"Roni is right!" called Old Eachann in his deep crackling voice, from the back of the crowd. "We need new songs, new stories, new rhymes."

"New songs, new stories, new rhymes," murmured Mr Voles.

"Plog is our only resident poet," rasped Roni, "but he cannot carry a tune, and he rarely leaves his bog."

The mice giggled, and Ruaridh twitched his whiskers. The young mouse who had cried "Bravo!" squeaked:

"Plog the frog,
  The Bard of the bog,
  Sits all agog,
  His mind in a fog;
  Croaks his old rhymes
  With a voice like a hog."

"That will be quite enough of that!" rasped Roni firmly. "Plog does his best, which is more than I can say for some folk," and she looked sternly at the mouse. Leaning forward, Roni whispered hoarsely in Algy's ear, "Actually, Plog's poems are not very good. But he does what he can."

"But he won't leave his bog," sniffed Ruaridh. "We need lots more stories and songs up here – here at the Singing Place. The bog's no place for a gathering!"

"No place for a gathering," agreed Mr Voles.

"Does Plog never come up here?" asked Algy.

"Old Eachann carries him up here in his beak on special occasions, but there's a wee problem with that," snuffled Ruaridh.

"Oh, yes," said Algy. "I heard about that."

"It makes Plog anxious," rasped Roni, "and then he doesn't perform well."

"I understand," said Algy.

"Don't misunderstand," rasped Roni. "Old Eachann is always a gentleman. He would never hurt Plog. But Plog is nervous."

"Poor Plog," said Algy, who still sympathized with the nervous frog.

"Plog's all right," snuffled Ruairidh, "but his songs all sound the same. We need new songs, and a new voice to sing them. New poems and stories and rhymes – and ballads!"

"Poems and stories and rhymes – and ballads! Poems and stories and rhymes – and ballads!" repeated Mr Voles eagerly.

"Won't you stay here and make up new songs for us?" snuffled Ruaridh.

"Well, I'd love to make up new songs for you," said Algy. "Making up songs is what a fluffy bird's supposed to do. I've been making up songs since I was a chick, but nobody wanted to hear them before."

"Perhaps your songs did not sound different to them," crackled the heron. "Maybe your stories were not new where you came from. But here they are new. Here they are different."

"Don't they like songs where you came from?" snuffled Ruaridh.

"They like songs very much," said Algy. "They just weren't interested in my songs. They said I was too young and too silly. There were lots of other fluffy birds there and they all made up songs, much better than mine."

"You don't say!" snuffled Ruaridh. "Lots of fluffy birds! But you'll stay here with us? Please stay! We have never had a fluffy bird here before. I'd be happy to help you find a new home, if you like."

Algy beamed at the friendly rabbit and jumped up onto his feet, accidentally flinging the startled Mr Voles off to one side. "Thank you!" he cried. "Thank you!" and he gave Ruaridh a large and exceedingly fluffy hug.

"My goodness!" exclaimed Roni, staring at Algy's fluffy white feathers, which were almost smothering the astonished rabbit.

Algy turned to the raven, and gave her a great big fluffy hug too.

"For goodness' sake!" gasped Roni, trying to smooth her feathers and get her breath back. "You certainly are an unusually fluffy bird, Algy. A surprisingly fluffy bird!"

"A sur-p-p-ris-ing-ly f-fluff-y b-b-bird" stuttered the shaken Mr Voles, from the rocky corner where he had been tossed.

"Fluffy Bird! Fluffy Bird! Surprise! Fluffy Bird!" a harsh voice screamed suddenly from behind Algy's head. Algy toppled backwards, and sat down on the rock with an uncomfortable bump.

"That's Calum MacCormac," snuffled Ruaridh, "one of the MacCormac brothers."

Leaning towards the rabbit, Algy whispered in his ear, "Is that the bird from the Black Rocks?"

"That's right," Ruaridh sniffed. "Craigie and Calum are the lookouts on the Black Rocks."

"Black Rocks! Black Rocks!" the cormorant shrieked, then quickly corrected himself. *"Fluffy Bird! Fluffy Bird! Surprise! Fluffy Bird!"*

"Excellent lookouts," rasped Roni, who had managed to recover her poise. "You can always hear their voices above the crashing of the waves."

"You certainly can," said Algy grimly, and he tried to smile at the fearsome, towering bird.

The cormorant nodded his head at Algy, as though in approval, and shrieked again, *"Fluffy Bird! Surprise! Fluffy Bird!"*

"Fluffy bird! Fluffy bird!" squeaked the chorus of mice, giggling at each other and wiggling their ears, and they started to chant in their high-pitched piping voices, "Fluffy, fluffy, fluffy, fluffy; bird, bird, fluffy bird."

"Fluffy, fluffy, fluffy, fluffy," murmured Mr Voles, as he crept back slowly towards Algy's foot.

Old Eachann stalked forward a few paces, and spoke again in his strange, deep voice. "Well, Algy?" he crackled. "What do you say? Will you stay here and make new songs for us? We need a fresh, new song-maker and poet. Your song was different. You have new songs to sing; new stories to tell. We would be pleased to hear your stories and your songs."

Algy looked at Old Eachann, and at Ruaridh and Roni and the giggling little mice. He looked across the crowd of expectant faces to the islands in the bay, and then out to sea, at the wide, dark ocean stretching far into the distance beyond. He looked down at the fuzzy Mr Voles, who was sitting beside his foot, and up at the bright blue sky, where Lark Lachlan was fluttering quietly just above him, waiting to hear what Algy would say.

"It all seems very strange to me. It's not at all like the place I came from, and I still don't know where I am," said Algy, and he paused. Mr Voles rubbed up against his foot anxiously, tickling Algy's leg with his whiskers.

"But of course I'll stay!" Algy cried, and springing up into the air he began to dance above the heads of the crowd at the Singing Place, flapping his wings excitedly and fluffing up his feathers. "Of course I'll stay! And I'll tell you new stories and make up new poems and songs for you. I'd be so happy to do that! Thank you! Thank you very much!"

"Thank you, Algy," crackled Old Eachann. "And welcome to your new home. May your stay here be a long and a happy one."

"A long and a happy one," echoed Mr Voles.

"Hooray!" shouted Ruaridh, and he thumped his foot vigorously on the ground again. "Hooray for Algy! Hooray for the fluffy bird!" And in a moment the whole crowd started cheering "Hooray for Algy! Hooray for the fluffy bird!" while Algy cavorted in the air above them, his fluffy white feathers ruffling up in all directions in the wind, and his dazzling yellow hair shining like fuzzy strands of gold in the sun.

"Fluffy," chuckled Mr Voles happily, stretching up against the rock as high as he could reach, to gaze at his new friend dancing in the sky. "Fluffy, fluffy bird!"

Lightning Source UK Ltd.
Milton Keynes UK
UKOW07f2340151015

260628UK00010B/35/P